SHE DOESN'T KNOW

Shane Morales

SHE DOESN'T KNOW

Copyright © 2017, 2018 Shane Morales

Third Edition
rev. date: 04/17/2018

ISBN: 154474980
ISBN-13: 978-1544749808

Xylem Flow Publishing

For Y,
who woke me up every morning.

CHAPTER ONE

"Who's that?" I asked Anna.

We'd just walked through the gravelly soccer field and were about to pass through the small gate into the housing area of the compound when I'd looked toward the basketball and volleyball courts to our right. There, making his way through the parking lot toward the commons, walked a boy, about my age, dressed in shorts and a blue tank top. There was something about the way he moved, his languid and fluid walk, like the laws of physics affected him differently than everyone else, that caught and held my attention. He was ... graceful.

He was too far away for me to make out his features, but I knew I hadn't seen him before.

Anna stopped, and she put her hand to her face to block the hot sun. I stopped next to her.

1

Anna was a few inches taller than me, willowy and lean, and had long, blonde hair that she held back in a high ponytail. She'd been the first kid to welcome me to my new home and had taken me around the compound to show me things and introduce me to people. That was just ten days ago, but already I felt close to her. She treated me like we'd known each other for years, and I felt pretty comfortable around her. As an Air Force Brat, I was used to being the new kid. While I was fine being alone and not fitting in—it had happened before—that wasn't something I'd choose over having friends. I'd been kind of anxious at first because the compound where I was now living was tiny. My mom told me there were something like five hundred people living here, and only a small number of kids my age. I'd been here at the compound ten days but had been introduced to just eight kids ranging in age from twelve to fourteen. They told me there'd been more kids last year, but most of them had moved back to the States at the end of the last school year. With so few kids, I'd been worried that they'd all be a tight clique and wouldn't want to hang out with the new kid, especially since none of them were military kids like me. So Anna's immediate acceptance had been a relief.

"That's Alex," she said as if he were a heavenly creature come down to earth to mix with the mortals. "I didn't think he'd be back this summer."

My eyes stayed fixed on Alex until he passed

behind the basketball court fence and out of sight. "What do you mean?"

We resumed our walk into the housing area, heading toward her house.

"He just finished ninth grade," she explained. "He's going to boarding school in Switzerland this year."

I'd heard of this. As an American kid living in Saudi, I would be going to an American school. A tiny school, just over in the small compound next to ours, but an American one. The school system here stopped at ninth grade. After that, you either moved back to the US with your family, or you went to boarding school. I was just about to enter ninth grade, and my parents had carefully explained that in a year, I might have to go to boarding school myself, depending on if my mom chose to stay in Saudi a second year.

"Do you know him well?" I asked as we walked down the street, houses on either side of us. One of the things about the compound that made it so different than anywhere else I'd lived was that, aside from color, the houses were identical. Two women in their late twenties or early thirties walked by us, and we waved to each other.

"Yeah," she said. "Since my sixth-grade year. We're pretty close. He's a nice guy. You'll like him." Anna was about to go into ninth grade, too, so that meant Alex had been in seventh grade when they met since he was a year ahead of us.

I hadn't realized Anna had been here so long.

"Were you two ever ... you know ... " I wasn't sure why I was asking, but I found myself more curious than I would have expected.

She laughed, shaking her head. "Oh no. Not us. He's been with other girls, but he's never looked at me that way. Which is fine. Last year we kissed at a party when we were playing spin the bottle, and it was really, really weird. Like kissing a brother or something. But you know Stacy?"

I nodded. Anna had introduced me to Stacy that first day she took me out to meet the other kids. Stacy was also going into ninth grade; she seemed okay, but there was something off about her that I couldn't quite put my finger on. I sort of felt like I had to watch what I said around her. She was a petite girl, with dark skin like she had a permanent tan, and her hair was sun-bleached and full bodied, falling over her shoulders in loose curls.

Anna continued as we approached her house. "Alex was with a girl named Callie last year—she was in his grade—but it's Stacy who's been with him the longest. They've been on and off again since I've known them. And to hear Stacy tell it, they messed around behind Callie's back last year, too. Which doesn't surprise me. She's ... experienced, if you know what I mean. And she's totally obsessed with him. Don't let her catch you making googly eyes at him or you'll end up on her bad side."

I made a face, blushing slightly as I wondered what "experienced" might mean. I mean, I knew what Anna meant, I just didn't know exactly how far that word suggested. Did it mean just kissing and stuff? Or going all the way? "I'm not going to make googly eyes at him, Anna. I don't even know him."

"Yeah, well, when you meet him you might have a change of heart. He's really cute."

I didn't reply because I was surprised at the little bit of excitement I felt at the thought of meeting Alex.

I had my first babysitting job that night. My mom, ever the popular and outgoing military wife, had made friends with other wives right away. One of them, a nice lady in her thirties, had two little kids and needed a babysitter for the evening. Since I'd been babysitting for a while, my mom had volunteered me.

So I'd shown up at Mrs. Werner's house in the early evening and was introduced to the husband—who told me to call him Sammy—and the kids. Jimmy was the oldest at four, and his little sister, Kira, was just three. Mrs. Werner had explained what the kids could and couldn't do, what I should feed them, what I should do in an emergency, and when bath and bed time were. Of course, she said not to have any boys over, which I thought was funny because there didn't seem to be boys around. Not that I'd met, anyway.

And that rule was broken a little over an hour later

when Anna showed up with Alex in tow. I'd answered the door to find them both standing there, Anna with a bright smile on her face, and Alex with his hands in the pockets of his shorts, looking like he didn't have a care in the world, with a sexy smile on his lips.

Anna had been totally right. He *was* cute. But it was his eyes ... his beautiful blue eyes that held me in place. They seemed to glow with an exciting energy that hinted at a wide-open love of life.

Anna didn't give me a chance to say anything. She pushed her way into the house, pulling Alex in behind her by the arm.

"Hey, girl!" she said. "I wanted you to meet Alex, so I brought him over." She watched me, and smirked.

Blushing, I looked over to Alex to see him looking back at me with that same alluring smile.

"Hi," he said in a warm, rich voice. "I'm Alex." He extended his hand.

After a few moments, Anna cleared her throat, and I realized with horror that I'd been staring at him. But ... wow, he was really cute. His dark, brown hair was a little bit too long, and his bangs lazily obscured his bright eyes. And that grin ... so sexy.

I wiped my hands on my shorts, hoping they weren't too sweaty, then shook his hand as confidently as I could. "Hi, Alex. I'm Chloe. It's nice to meet you."

"Likewise," he said. A few seconds passed. "I ... uh ... kind of need my hand back."

Oh god

I let go of his hand and turned away, so he couldn't tell how badly I was blushing. There was no hiding it from Anna, though. She leaned in close to me. "Told you," she whispered. Then she went to the hall and shouted, "Jimmy! Kira! Uncle Alex is here!"

There was a commotion of toys being abandoned from the bedroom where I'd left the kids, and soon Jimmy and Kira came running out with goofy, little-kid grins and huge, bright eyes.

"Alex!" They came running over and threw themselves at his legs, Kira reaching up so he could pick her up.

I was surprised. I didn't expect him to know the kids, and I didn't expect them to be so obviously in love with him.

Anna made a petulant face and said to me, "They like him better than me." Her pout turned into a grin as she watched the kids.

Alex had a wide smile on his face as he scooped Kira up in his arms and rubbed Jimmy's head. "Hey, guys," he said to them. "How's it shaking?" he asked in a knowing, secretive tone.

There was more squealing, and Kira wriggled in Alex's arms until he put her down. She and Jimmy both turned around and stuck their butts out to him.

"Show me what you got!" Alex said to them, crossing his arms over his chest and looking official, like he was about to judge an event.

Immediately, Jimmy and Kira began to dance,

shaking their rear ends and pumping their arms wildly.

Anna laughed out loud, and I watched, entranced, at how much these two little kids seemed to adore Alex. Then my eyes widened, and a little laugh escaped me when Alex jumped forward and began to dance with them although he refrained from wiggling his butt . The three of them danced together until the kids fell to the floor giggling.

Again, I was surprised. Alex didn't seem to care at all that he was dancing like a goof and badly in front of a girl he'd just met. I liked that he was comfortable enough with himself to do something like that. He was confident, and I found that attractive.

Suddenly Jimmy jumped up. "Alex! Come see what I got!" Then he ran back down the hall toward the bedrooms.

Kira ran after Jimmy. "Me too!"

"I'll be back," Alex said to us, then followed the kids down the hall like he lived here himself.

Anna and I watched him go.

I turned back to Anna to find her smirking at me. "And you said you wouldn't make googly eyes at him."

"He's ... " I managed, not really sure what to say.

Anna patted my shoulder. "Yeah, I know. He's ... Alex."

"I guess the kids know him pretty well," I said, wanting to get the attention off of me.

"He used to live next door," she explained. "We've both known the kids since they were teeny-tiny."

I made a face, and Anna's smile faded. "What is it?"

"It's just that Mrs. Werner said not to have any boys over."

Anna waved her hand at me. "Don't worry. The parents love Alex. They won't care that he's over. Just don't get caught half-naked on the sofa with him when they get home. That might bother them."

"Anna! That will *not* happen!"

She smirked again. "You said you wouldn't make googly eyes at him either, and you didn't even last five seconds."

"That's totally different!"

"Relax, Chloe," she said, stepping toward the hall. "I'm teasing. It's just that you look so amazed it's actually kind of cute. We better go check on them before Alex has the kids dismantling the furniture to build a fort."

CHAPTER TWO

Two hours later, after Alex had played with the kids for a while, and after I'd fed them, given them baths, and put them to bed, I realized Anna was nowhere to be found.

I searched the house and then came into the living room to find Alex sitting on the sofa, looking through a *National Geographic*. He looked up at me expectantly.

"Where's Anna?" I asked him, still looking around like maybe she was hiding somewhere that I'd neglected to look.

"Oh," he said, putting the magazine down. "She left while you were putting the kids to bed."

I just stared at him, wondering why she hadn't said anything, and why Alex hadn't left with her.

I guess Alex could see the confusion on my face because he said, "She said you wanted to talk to me about something."

I groaned. *That Anna* I was going to kill her. And now I'd have to think of something to talk about or else I'd just stand there in front of him looking like an idiot. "I ... um ... well ... "

He laughed like he'd just realized what Anna had done. "You didn't really want to talk to me about something, did you?"

"Um ... no?" I didn't know what else to say.

He put the magazine back on the coffee table. "Should I go?"

It burst out of me before I could think about it. "No! I mean ... you could stay. If you wanted to. I don't mind."

"Okay," he said, a gentle smile on his face, as he relaxed back into the sofa cushions. Then he gave me that lopsided grin that I was beginning to like so much. "Are you just going to stand there?" He nodded toward the other end of the sofa.

I blushed, again, realizing that I'd been staring at him. Again.

hat is wrong with me?

"Oh. Yeah. I'll just ... I'll just sit over here." I made my way around the coffee table and sat on the sofa, keeping a full cushion between us.

And sat there like an idiot because I didn't know what to say. Which annoyed me because I usually didn't have a hard time talking to people. Okay, sure, Alex was gorgeous, but I'd been around cute boys before, and I'd never let them affect me like this. What was it about him that made me so ...

"I make you nervous," he finally said to me.

"No. It's just ... I don't ... a little bit." I looked down at my hands because I didn't know what else to do, and groaned inwardly. Why was I admitting that to him? And why couldn't I seem to talk in complete sentences?

"I don't bite, you know."

"I know." I risked turning my head so I could look at him, knowing that my cheeks must be flaming.

Alex turned slightly and brought his left leg under him so he could face me better. "Here's what we're going to do. First I'm going to ask you simple questions about yourself. Then you'll ask them back to me. We'll talk for a bit and, hopefully, you won't be so nervous. Then I'll ask you more personal questions—to get to know you better—and if you're interested, you can ask about me. Sound good?"

I nodded, caught between relief and annoyance at how he was taking control of the conversation. I wanted to tell him no, that I was fully capable of having a conversation without being led by the hand, but all I managed to get out was, "Okay."

"All right," he said, shifting in his seat again. "Here we go. How long have you been here?"

Okay Relax, Chloe Just answer the questions Use your big words

"Ten days," I said, still feeling annoyingly awkward.

"And where were you before?"

"Arizona. Glendale. My dad was stationed at Luke Air Force Base. He's a captain." Dad was a flight instructor. He was here in Saudi to train the Saudis how to fly fighter jets.

"Oh yeah?" he said with interest. "Cool. I was born in Arizona. How long did you live there?"

"Two years."

He nodded slightly and leaned against the cushion, getting more comfortable. "Did you have lots of friends there?"

I raised a shoulder, let it drop. "Not really. Just a few. It's hard to make friends when you know you're going to leave them in a year or two."

Okay, that's better. Just keep talking.

"That makes sense," he said. "How big was your school?"

"Pretty big, I guess. There were a couple hundred kids there."

He laughed. "Wow, I can't even imagine that. It's not like that here. Do you know how many kids will be in your class this year?"

"Anna says it will be something like eight. I haven't met everyone yet. I think some kids are still on vacation." Now that I seemed to be able to talk, I began to feel less nervous.

"Probably. There were eleven of us in my ninth-grade class. Most of them moved back to the States, though. It's just me, Logan, Hudson, and London left.

We're all going to boarding school. They should be in any day now, so you'll get to meet them."

I didn't recognize the names. Anna hadn't mentioned them. "Are they all your friends?"

"Yeah. Hudson is my best friend. And I'm pretty tight with London. Okay, now it's your turn."

"Right." I took in a small breath. *You can do this* I started with something easy. "How long have you lived here?"

"Since 1981," he replied. His eyes never left mine, and I looked right back at him, taking in his gorgeous face. "I moved here when I was in fifth grade. The compound hadn't even been built yet. We had to live in a building in the city, and we went to a different school. I was one of the original kids here. I think it's only me and Hudson who are left from that time."

Wow, that was a long time ago. I found myself imagining him as a cute little fifth-grader. Had he worn scuffed up jeans with holes in the knees? A lopsided baseball cap? Had his hair been messy? And had his smile been as cute as it was now?

"Is that why Hudson is your best friend?" I asked.

"One of the reasons. I've known him longer than anyone, so we have a lot of history together. He's just a good guy, and I know he always has my back."

There was a bit of a lull, but Alex just looked at me expectantly, like I should continue.

"Where did you live before you came here?" I managed after a few moments of silence.

"Ecuador. I moved there when I was in second grade."

"Wow. So you pretty much grew up overseas."

"Yeah." He grinned again, and it made my heart flutter. "All I know about being a kid in the US is from movies."

That made me stop for a moment because Alex seemed to have an even stranger life than mine. Sure I moved around a lot, but I'd always lived somewhere in the States. Alex hadn't lived in America since he was a little kid. "It's not that glamorous," I told him. "I was bored most of the time."

He laughed at that. "Yeah, right. You'll really get to know what boring is after you've been here for a while. There's nothing to do here."

I wasn't sure what to say to that, and a quiet settled over us.

"Are you still nervous?" he asked after a few moments.

My eyebrows raised slightly, and my lips curled up in a half-smile when I realized that I felt pretty comfortable. "No."

"Good," he said, grinning. "Now I'm going to ask you more personal questions. Ready?"

"Yes."

"How old are you?"

"Fourteen," I replied.

"When is your birthday?"

"July 28."

"Oh. So you just turned fourteen last month. Mine's May 9. That means I'm ... " He looked up and began counting off with his fingers. It was cute. "That means I'm fourteen months older than you."

That made sense, what with him being a year ahead of me.

"You're fifteen then," I said to him.

"Yep. So," he continued, "what are you into?"

"You mean, what do I like to do?"

"Yeah. Hobbies and stuff."

"I like to read," I said, shrugging. "And I draw."

"Oh yeah? What sort of stuff do you read?"

"Fantasy mostly."

His smile grew wider. "Really? Me too. Have you read *The Hobbit* and *The Lord of the Rings*?"

I nodded, feeling a little flutter in my chest. I'd never met anyone who was into fantasy before. Could he be any more perfect? "Yes. Last year. I love them."

"What else have you read? The Shannara books?"

"Yes!" I replied excitedly. "I love those books. The end of *The Elfstones of Shannara* made me cry so hard."

He let out a small, amused laugh. "Yeah, me too a little. Do you have lots of books?"

I shook my head. "No. Just a few of my favorites. I move around too much to have lots of books. I was hoping the library here would have some fantasy books, but when I looked for them, they were all missing."

He laughed again. "That's because I stole them all."

"You stole them?" I asked, surprised and a little annoyed. Who steals books from a library? "What if other people wanted them? Like me?"

"Relax," he said, putting up his hands. "Trust me when I tell you I was the only person reading them. You're the only other person I've met here that's shown any interest. So what do you like to draw?"

"Stuff I read in books," I answered. "But mostly things I imagine in my head."

"Cool. Do you think I can see some of your drawings?"

I liked how he assumed that we would hang out again. It made that fluttery feeling grow stronger. "Maybe. So what do you like to do? I already know you like to steal books. What else is there?"

"I like to write," he said simply.

"Really? What do you write? Fantasy?"

"Mostly."

"Have you been doing that long?"

"About two years."

"Will you let me read some of it?" I asked.

His smile faded a little bit. "Sorry. I don't share it with anyone. It's just a thing for me. Like a journal. It's private."

"Oh. I guess I'll just have to wonder," I said, trying to tease because I wanted him to smile again.

We ended up talking for a while. I asked Alex more questions about himself, finding that I wanted to know more and more about him, and the more we talked, the more my nerves settled down. When he spoke, I watched him closely, taking in his amazing eyes and great smile. A wonderful tingle shot through me, reminding me that I was talking to a really cute boy who I was liking more and more.

Then the door opened, and I shot up, panicked, like I'd been caught doing something really bad.

Sammy and Mrs. Werner stepped into the living room, and I could see the disappointment on Mrs. Werner's face. "Chloe, I thought I told you—"

But then her frown disappeared when Alex stepped out into view.

"Alex!" She seemed genuinely happy. "So nice to see you again! I didn't know you'd come back. I wasn't sure if we'd see you again before you left for boarding school."

Sammy interrupted. "I'm going to check on the kids. Nice to see you, Alex." Then he disappeared down the hall.

"Hi, Janet," Alex said, and I didn't miss that he used her first name. Anna was right. Mrs. Werner must really like Alex to let him address her by her first name. "I just came in last night. Anna brought me over to meet the new girl. I hope that was okay."

Mrs. Werner walked to the dining room, put her purse on the table and rummaged through it. "Of course! You should know that you're always welcome here, Alex. The kids love you like an older brother.

They must have been excited to see you."

"Yeah, we had some fun," he said.

Mrs. Werner pulled out some money from her purse and held it out to me. "Here you are, Chloe. There's a little bit extra there. Consider it a retainer. How were the kids?"

I took the cash and briefly summarized the evening, and she seemed satisfied.

"Thanks again, Chloe. I'll call your mother when we need you again." She waved me toward the living room and the front door. "Go on. Go do whatever it is you kids do. Have fun."

Once outside, I stood alone with Alex, not sure what to do or say.

"Hey, do you want to hang out a bit at the commons?" he asked. "There's bound to be someone at the snack bar or something." The commons was the part of the compound where all the facilities—things like the rec center, the sports courts and fields, the pool, and the dining hall and snack bar—were located. It was where I'd been hanging out with Anna most evenings.

"I'm sorry," I said. "I'm supposed to go home."

"Oh. Well, can I walk you home then?"

"Sure," I said as butterflies fluttered in my stomach. "That would be nice."

It only took a couple of minutes to get to my house because I lived just one street over so we didn't really talk.

"I'll see you around, okay?" he said, standing at the street in front of my house, as I made my way up the walkway to my front patio.

"Yeah. I'll probably be out with Anna tomorrow."

"'Kay, I'll look for you. It was nice to meet you, Chloe."

That warm, fluttery feeling filled my chest again, and I smiled. "It was nice to meet you too. Good night."

"Good night." He turned and walked away.

I watched him until he was out of sight, then I walked into my house with the realization that I had a huge crush.

CHAPTER THREE

I stayed up pretty late reading, so it was almost ten a.m. when my Mom came into my room and woke me up.

"Honey," she said. "It's time to get up." She went over to the window by the bed and threw open the drapes. Sunlight streamed into my room, making me shut my eyes for a moment. "There's a nice boy waiting for you in the living room," she said with a twinkle in her eye.

I sat straight up. *Oh my gosh!*

"Who is it?" I asked, even though I already knew.

Mom walked over to the door and looked back at me. "His name is Alex. He says you two met yesterday. Now take a shower and get dressed and I'll have breakfast ready for you. I'll keep your guest entertained." She left the room and closed the door.

I immediately jumped out of bed and rummaged through my dresser looking for something nice to wear. I didn't want to get too dressed up—it was just a regular summer day—but I didn't want to wear something too ratty looking either.

After a quick shower, and after putting on some light makeup I was so glad Mom let me use makeup , I walked down the hall toward the living room. I could hear Mom talking to Alex about me.

"Oh, yes," she said to him from the kitchen. "She was a bumblebee in her second-grade production. She had chubby cheeks back then, and she looked so cute. I have pictures. I'll just bring them out—"

I stepped into the kitchen. "Mom! Will you stop embarrassing me?" God, who knew what mortifying things she'd been telling Alex? I groaned at the thought.

"It's a mother's prerogative to embarrass her daughter, sweetie. But, fine, I'll keep quiet. Alex is waiting for you."

I found Alex sitting at the dining table, dressed in shorts and a tank top. My heart did a little flip, and a goofy smile spread across my face.

"Hey, Chloe," he said, smiling brightly at me. "How's it going? Sleep well?"

"Hi, Alex" I replied, trying to keep the excitement from my voice. "I did. Thanks."

Mom came from the kitchen with a plate of pancakes. "Alex has been telling me the most interesting stories about his time here. Did you know he's lived here for five years?"

I sat at the table, noticing that it was set for two. "I

did, actually. We talked yesterday."

Mom went back into the kitchen and came back with a plate of beef sausages man, I was going to miss pork and syrup. She had a half-amused, half-disapproving look on her face. "Yes. Janet called, and she let slip that she found you and Alex in her house. If she hadn't assured me that she didn't mind and that Alex is an outstanding young man, you and I would be having words, young lady." She put the plate of sausages between us. "Now dig in before it gets cold. Alex, eat all you want. I know how growing boys eat their weight in food every day."

"Yes, ma'am," he said. "Thank you."

Mom looked at him, smiling. "Such a nice boy," she cooed and then went back to the kitchen.

I wasn't surprised to see that Alex had charmed my mom. I had the feeling that even the grumpiest parents would find him endearing. He just had a way about him that made you want to like him.

Whatever it was, it was certainly working on me.

"I didn't know if you'd be up yet, so I waited a while before coming over," he said. "I don't usually get up this early during the summer, but my sleep schedule is pretty messed up right now. I've been up for hours."

I took the plate of pancakes from him and forked the remaining two onto my plate. "I don't usually sleep this late," I told him. "I was up late reading. Um ... not that I'm not glad you're here, but why did you come over?"

He reached down and pulled up a large paper bag. "I brought you gifts," he explained, then put the bag back down on the floor.

My curiosity was piqued. What could he have brought me? I was dying to know, but I didn't ask about it. I just sat there and ate quietly.

Alex turned his attention to his food while I sneaked glances at him. He had good table manners, eating his food calmly and carefully. Despite that, though, he looked very happy to be eating a big meal.

"What?" he asked, and I realized I'd been staring at him again.

I quickly looked away. "Nothing," I said, hoping he'd drop it.

He did, and we ate in silence.

When we were finished eating, Alex helped me clear the table and bring everything into the kitchen, where Mom was unpacking tangerines from a big box and arranging them in a basket. She shooed me away as I turned the sink faucet on. "I've got this, honey. Go entertain your guest."

"Okay. Thanks. We'll be in my room."

She turned at that and pinned me with a look. "The door stays open."

I groaned. She just wasn't going to let that go, was she? And did she have to say that right in front of Alex?

In my room with the door open , I sat on my bed as Alex looked around, taking in my room.

"Wow," he said. "You don't have posters up or anything. Don't you have girly things to decorate with?"

I shrugged. "Um ... no ... I haven't felt like decorating yet. And most of my stuff still hasn't arrived." Whenever I moved to a new place, I always waited a few weeks before decorating because I liked to get a feel for my new home before deciding what to put up. "So what did you bring me?"

"Oh yeah," he said like he'd forgotten that he was holding the paper bag. He held it out to me.

I took it and opened it up. It was packed full of books. I reached in and took one out. It was a library book.

"Are these all the books you stole from the library?"

"Yep. I've read them all, and since I'm going to be leaving soon, I didn't want them just sitting in my room. I figured you'd want them."

"Oh." I reached into the bag and pulled out more books. The ones at the top were the Xanth series by Piers Anthony. I'd always wanted to read those. "Thank you." I was giddy knowing that Alex had been thinking of me.

"No problem," he said, running his hand through his hair, leaving it a bit messy. I had an almost overwhelming need to reach out and fix it. "Just don't tell your parents where they came from."

"Don't worry," I said, putting the books back in

the bag. "I'll keep them hidden. Until I've read them anyway. Then I'll probably return them to the library."

Until I've read them anyway. Then I'll probably return them to the library."

"You're such a good girl," he said with a grin.

I blushed. "I can be bad if I want," I lied. I wasn't a bad girl. The worst thing I'd ever done was get caught making out with Sam Peterson on my bed during my thirteenth birthday party. Mom had yelled, Sam had cried, and I'd been utterly humiliated. Then she'd sat me down, and we had a mortifying talk about sex. That was when Mom started the "door stays open" rule.

"Yeah, I'll believe that when I see it." He glanced over at my desk. "Is that one of your drawings?" he asked and moved over to the desk.

I jumped up, grabbing my papers. "They're not finished."

He laughed. "I won't mind. I just want to see some of your stuff."

"Well ... " I turned around and leafed through the papers, finding one that was almost finished. I pulled it out and handed it to him.

He took the paper, and his eyes widened.

"Holy crap, Chloe. This is awesome. Who is she?"

I'd drawn an elf girl, dressed in flowing silk, standing by a magic portal, and a tiny dragon perched on her shoulder. She was looking right out of the drawing, right into your eyes.

"I call her Serres," I said. "She's an Elven sorceress. That's her familiar. He's a pseudo-dragon."

He studied my drawing. "This is amazing, Chloe. You're really good."

My cheeks heated as I blushed, pleased beyond words at his compliment. "Thank you."

He handed the paper back to me. "Will you show me some more later?"

"Maybe," I said, and moved to the desk where I put the papers in the top drawer. "When I finish some, sure."

"Hey," he said. "I was going to hang out at the pool. Do you want to come?"

Oh my gosh. Was I ready to for him to see me in a bathing suit? Sure, it was pretty tame for a bikini, but it would show off my body, and somehow that scared me. Which was ridiculous. I'd been in a bathing suit around boys before, plenty of times. Why would it be any different with Alex?

I tried not to admit it to myself, but I knew it for the truth. I was scared because I cared what he thought of me. I wanted him to think I looked okay. I wanted him to think I was attractive.

"Sure," I finally said. "Will Anna be there?"

"No. She said she was going out shopping in the city with her parents."

"Oh. Well, just let me get changed. Wait for me in the living room, okay?"

CHAPTER FOUR

It was a beautiful, hot day, without a cloud in the sky. Despite the heat, the humidity was low because we were about six thousand feet in elevation. The heat could get really bad at sea level. When we first stepped out of the airport in Jeddah, which was on the Red Sea, the humidity was crushing, and it felt like we were moving through water. It was impossibly hot. I was glad it was much cooler and drier in Taif.

It was just before eleven o'clock when Alex and I arrived at the pool. We pretty much had it to ourselves. There was only a young mother with her two kids over by the kiddie pool.

The pool itself was large, maybe even bigger than an Olympic pool, but there wasn't a diving board, which I was kind of bummed about.

Alex and I laid out our towels on lounge chairs by the deep end, across from the snack bar and locker rooms. Behind us was a large pavilion that stretched down the length of both pools, providing shade over metal picnic benches.

Somewhat self-consciously, I took off my top, then slid out of my shorts. I stood there, feeling exposed, while Alex looked at the pool as if he were contemplating just jumping in.

Then he reached down to the hem of his shirt and pulled it off.

And then I didn't know where to look.

Holy bananas! I'd already seen his lean arms and nice biceps, but now his chest and stomach were on display. He was lean, but his chest muscles were full, and the muscles of his shoulders rippled under his tanned skin. Most striking, though, were his defined abs. He even had the V that slanted down and disappeared into his shorts. My hormones filled me deep in my belly, and heat scorched my face as I blushed furiously. I could hardly believe the thoughts I was having. I'd never been attracted to a boy in that way before.

I looked away, hoping he hadn't noticed me ogling his body. I didn't want to be caught staring at him again.

"So do you want to jump in or warm up in the sun a little bit first?" he asked, standing there, awaiting my answer.

"I ... let's lay out a bit first." I took out my lotion from my bag, sat down, and started applying it to my arms and legs. When I started on my shoulders and stomach, Alex stepped closer.

"Do you want me to do your back?" he asked, and from his tone and the innocent look on his face, he wasn't being creepy.

I hesitated at first, but then, with a growing confidence, and a bit of flirty excitement, I said, "Okay. Thanks." Then I turned my back to him and reached behind me to hold up my hair.

I waited for a few seconds as he squeezed lotion into his palm, then held in a small gasp as his hands touched me and began moving all over my back. Exhilaration ran through me, making my toes tingle and my skin flush. My heart fluttered at his touch.

When he was done, I let my hair down.

"There," he said, handing me back the lotion. "You're good."

He had no idea how good I was. I wanted him to touch me more, for hours and hours.

"Thank you," I said, surprised I was able to speak coherently.

I waited as he dragged his lounge chair closer and then reclined on it. Then I leaned back in my chair and lay there quietly, enjoying the flush of heat I was feeling from the warming sun.

After a bit of silence, he spoke. "This is pretty much all there is to do here during the summer. Even after school starts you'll probably be spending a lot of time here. At least until they close the pool in October."

"Oh yeah?" I'd only been to the pool twice in the ten days since I arrived, but that was mostly because there weren't really any kids to hang out with. The first time I'd come was with my mom, and only Anna and Stacy had come later. Then I came back a few days later with Anna. But I could see that Alex was right. There wasn't much else to do.

"Definitely," Alex said. "During the summer we basically live here. If I hadn't been in the States all summer, I'd have been here every day."

"So what do you do at night?" I asked.

"Depends."

"On what?"

"On whether or not we have alcohol."

I snapped my head toward him. "Alcohol? You drink?"

"Sure," he replied simply as if it had been a silly question. "A lot of us do. It's just something else to do."

I was confused. "But I thought alcohol was illegal here."

"It is," he answered. "But people make their own. Mostly this stuff called sadiki, which I think is a type of moonshine. It's really harsh."

Moonshine? I was amazed. He was talking about drinking hard alcohol like it was nothing. Was this normal here?

"How do you get it?" I asked, curious.

"We go out in the middle of the night sometimes

and sneak into people's houses and steal it. Sometimes some of the younger single guys who live up in camp three get us a case of stuff, and we hide it."

The housing area of the compound was split into three distinct sections, called camps. Camp three was farthest from the commons, at the far west end of the compound, and the single men all lived there. My mom had told me not to go there, which was fine because I had no reason to.

"Do you want to try it?" he asked. His tone was as if he was asking if I wanted to try a new flavor of ice cream. How could he be so casual about this?

My eyes widened. "Uh ... no thanks." My parents would absolutely kill me if they even suspected I was drinking. I couldn't even imagine it. Back home there'd been rumors of some of the bad kids getting caught drinking, but I never really believed them. I mean, we were in middle school. We were way too young to be drinking.

But that didn't seem to be the case here. Alex talked about drinking like it was something he did all the time and had been doing for a while.

"When did you first start drinking?" I asked, hoping I wasn't being too nosy.

He shrugged, looking out over the pool. "When I was twelve, I guess. Hudson and I went with some older kids over the compound walls, and we all drank a bottle of Jim Beam. Man, that was a riot. I was drunk for two days."

Holy bananas! I couldn't believe it. Twelve? I couldn't imagine kids that young drinking alcohol. That was crazy!

I felt a little bit weird after that, so I kept quiet.

Alex seemed to settle in. He laced his fingers together and placed his hands on his sexy stomach. I couldn't tell if his eyes were open because of his dark sunglasses, but I imagined they were closed.

So we lay on our lounge chairs together, silently. I was still reeling about the alcohol.

About twenty minutes later, Alex sat up and took his sunglasses off.

"I'm going in," he said. "Want to come in with me?"

I was nice and warm, so I nodded. "Okay."

Alex didn't wait for me. He took a couple of running steps and launched himself into the air, making a big splash as he hit the water. His head emerged a few moments later, and he waved at me. "Come on," he urged. "It's great."

I stepped up to the edge of the pool, took in a breath and dove into the water. It was so nice. The water was cool, but not cold, and felt great on my warm skin.

I surfaced next to Alex, a grin on my face.

"Told you," he said, grinning back at me. "Hey, do you want to race? We can warm up."

"I've been on the swim team most of my life," I told him. "I think I could take you."

"That sounds like a challenge," he replied with a flirty look in his eyes.

"Maybe it was," I flirted back.

"Okay. I accept your challenge. Come on."

We swam over to the edge of the pool by the deep end.

"One lap," he said, pointing to the other end of the pool. "There and back. Loser buys soda."

"You're on."

We clung to the side of the pool.

"Ready ... set ... go!"

And we were off. I swam hard, but not so much that I would lose steam. I wanted to pace myself.

Alex immediately surged ahead of me, and he started to pull away. He stayed ahead of me most of the length of the pool, but as we neared the other side, he began to slow. He flipped first, a few seconds ahead of me, and when I did too, I swam with more force. Soon I was catching up to him. About midway to the deep end, I passed him, and with my last remaining strength, I pushed ahead, leaving him behind.

I hit the wall at least two seconds ahead of him.

When he caught up, he shook his head to get his wet hair out of his face, and he laughed. "Holy crap, Chloe!" he said excitedly between gasps of air. "And I thought I was fast. You blew right by me!"

If I hadn't already been flushed by the exertion, I would have blushed at his praise.

"Let that be a lesson to you," I said, grinning, and

splashed a bit of water at him.

He laughed again, giving me his brilliant, beautiful smile that made me all gooey inside.

"I need a break after that," Alex said, then pulled himself out of the pool. "What type of soda do you want?"

"Mirinda, please."

"'Kay, I'll be right back."

While I waited for Alex to come back from the snack bar, I floated in the water on my back, thinking about the enigma that was Alex. On the one hand, he seemed like a sweet boy who was gentle and charming, and everyone seemed to like him. I liked that Alex. A lot. But he stole books from the library and drank alcohol. That was the sort of behavior I'd expect from bad kids who were always getting in trouble. Which was the real Alex? The sweet boy I had a serious crush on, or the bad kid who stole and drank?

Soon Alex came out of the snack bar and walked toward our lounge chairs with two cans of soda and a paper plate.

"Come on," he said as he passed me. "I got some fries, too."

I got out of the water and after drying off with my towel, I followed him. We sat together at a picnic table near our lounge chairs while we ate and drank soda. Alex seemed content to keep silent, but he would occasionally give me a goofy grin, and I would smile shyly back at him.

When we were finished, Alex led me back to the lounge chairs, and he reclined fully on his. I laid out on mine, staying silent and sometimes sneaking glances at him.

Maybe half an hour later two kids I didn't recognize, a boy and a girl, walked through the gates of the pool area by the snack bar. They stood there for a second, then the girl called out.

"Alex!"

Alex sat up and his gaze settled on the new arrivals.

Instantly, he was up and running toward them. The boy hung back, but the girl ran to meet him, her laughter ringing out.

They crashed into each other mid-way, arms entangled in a tight hug like they were lovers who hadn't seen each other in years. Alex lifted her up off the ground and spun her around as she laughed, clinging tightly to him. Then she kissed him on the cheek and stepped away.

I watched, surprised at the jealousy I felt.

The boy approached Alex and the girl, and he and Alex hugged in that back-slapping way guys do. They spoke for a few moments, then Alex pointed in my direction, and they started walking toward me.

I waited for them.

As they approached, I studied the new kids, especially the girl.

She was stunning. She looked older, more mature than someone our age. Her hair was long and straight, a platinum blonde that was almost white, and held back in a high ponytail. Even from where I sat, I could see the brilliance of her green eyes. She wore jean shorts and a red T-shirt. A bag hung from her shoulders.

The boy was about the same height and build as Alex, but his hair was sandy and cut shorter. He was cute but not as good looking as Alex. A towel was draped over his neck.

When they arrived at our area, they stopped talking, and Alex motioned toward me.

"Guys, this is Chloe," he said in his bright, friendly voice. "She's new here. She's going into ninth grade." Then he turned his attention to me. "Chloe, this is London and Hudson. They're my best buds."

"Hi," I said, feeling a bit intimidated, and not liking it. "It's nice to meet you."

London stepped forward and grabbed my hands. "Hi, Chloe! It's so nice to meet you." Then, surprisingly, she embraced me in a hug.

When she pulled away, Hudson reached out with a hand. "Hey," he said. "Glad to meet you."

I grabbed his hand and shook it, relieved that he wasn't going to hug me, even if he seemed to be a nice guy.

"We figured you'd be at the pool," London said as she dragged a chaise closer to us. "Looks like we were right."

"When did you guys get in?" Alex asked.

"Late last night," London replied, spreading out

her towel.

"I got in this morning," Hudson added, as he grabbed a lounge chair, too.

"Any word from Logan?" Alex asked as he sat on his chair.

Hudson spread out his towel before answering. "He sent a postcard a few weeks ago. He said he was coming in before we go to Switzerland, but he wasn't sure about the date."

"Where was he?" London asked.

"California."

I simply watched them in silence, feeling awkward and uncomfortable, like an outsider. So I sat down on my lounge chair and took sips from my soda as they got settled in.

When London undressed, I watched in amazement.

She wore a small, red string bikini that showed off more skin that I would have felt comfortable baring. And her body ... I could hardly believe it. Yes, she looked older with clothes on but dressed only in her bikini, with her body on display, it was apparent that she really *was* more mature. She had the body of a grown woman, with large, full breasts, a slim waist, and curvy hips. Clearly, she'd grown into her body at an early age.

She made me feel like a twelve-year-old boy, and I didn't like it. I *really* wanted not to like her.

I looked toward Alex to gauge his reaction, but he

didn't seem to notice the beautiful, practically naked girl standing next to him. I wasn't sure what to make of that.

After London and Hudson got settled, they turned their attention to me.

"So," London began, a warm, pleasant smile on her face. "Chloe, have you been here long?"

I answered her questions, much like I had with Alex. At first, I was intimidated by this beautiful girl-woman, but she was so friendly and easygoing that I soon began to feel comfortable. She asked all sorts of questions about me—where I had lived, about my old school, if I had any siblings, what sorts of things I liked to do, and what I thought about living in the compound.

My gaze kept flitting to Alex, wondering if I'd catch him ogling London, but when he looked at her he kept his gaze on her face.

Were they so close that London's sexuality wasn't an issue between them?

An hour or so later, Stacy and her best friend, Avery, arrived. Alex called out to them, and they came over. When they all greeted each other, Stacy and London were cool toward each other at best. Something was definitely going on there.

"Hi, London," Avery said and stopped by London's feet. "How are you?" There wasn't much expression on her face—which was something I was beginning to see was normal for her—but her eyes were intense.

Avery was average height like me, and she had dirty blonde hair that hung in slight waves to her shoulders. Her blue eyes were big and dominated her pretty face that was graced by a sprinkle of light freckles. She was quiet, saying little, and I got the feeling that she watched everything.

"Oh," London said, becoming quiet. "Um ... hi, Avery. Hi. I...um...yeah, I'm good. You?"

Was she nervous?

Avery's lips curled up slightly. "Just fine." Then she left us and rejoined Stacy. The two of them laid out their towels on the ground, then they both dove into the pool where they stayed for at least half an hour before they came back out and laid out on the ground, keeping to themselves for the most part.

A few hours later, I felt like I'd had too much sun, and started to get a little bit sleepy. I was trying to figure out a way to politely excuse myself without seeming like I was running away, when Alex asked the group, "What are we doing later?"

"I have to take a nap," Hudson said. "I'm still on US time."

"I have to unpack," London added. "And I need a shower. But I'm open to anything."

"Hey," Hudson said. "Do you guys want to get something from the stash and drink?"

Oh no They were going to drink. There was no way I could be part of that.

Alex looked over to me and held my gaze for a few seconds. Then he said, "Nah. I don't feel like it. How about we hang out at Chloe's?"

I raised my eyebrows in surprise. He was making sure I was included and that we wouldn't be doing something I wasn't comfortable with. I smiled at him in appreciation, happy beyond words that we was thinking of me like that.

He winked back at me.

"Well," I began, "we could maybe play a board game? I can grill burgers for us or something."

"Oh man," Hudson said longingly, "grilled burgers ... that sounds good to me."

"Yeah, let's do that," London added as she stood up, then began dressing.

Hudson and Alex stood too and put on their shirts.

Feeling like an idiot for just watching them, I stood and put on my own clothes.

"Is six o'clock okay for you guys?" I asked.

Hudson and Alex laughed.

"I'll have to check my busy schedule," Alex said teasingly, "but if I move my appointments around I may be able to pencil it in." He winked at me again, and I felt a little bit foolish.

"Yeah, six works for me," Hudson said.

He and London said goodbye, leaving Alex and me standing there.

I realized that I hadn't invited Stacy and Avery, and

I felt very rude for not including them. So I looked over at them and caught Stacy's attention. "Can you guys come, too?"

Stacy and Alex looked at each other as if they were having a silent conversation. Then, after something had clearly been decided between them, Alex glanced away.

"Yeah, maybe," Stacy eventually said.

"Okay. Well, see you then," I said awkwardly. I said bye to Alex and then left them, feeling like I had missed something important.

CHAPTER FIVE

Late that afternoon, I got the plates and glasses ready, stocked the cooler with ice and soda, and helped Mom prepare the food. When I'd told her what I'd wanted to do, she seemed very pleased that I had made friends and was eager to help out.

"So," I carefully began while I was cutting tomato slices. "I think I can grill these up on my own. You know, if you and Dad have plans or anything."

Mom stepped out from behind the fridge door and bumped it shut with her hip. "You're not very subtle, you know. If you want the house to yourself, just say so."

"Would it matter if I did?"

She handed me a plastic container to put the tomato slices in. "Who did you say is coming over?"

"Anna and Alex. And Stacy and Avery, too. And two friends of Alex's who just came in today. I met them at the pool earlier."

"Chloe, I don't really like the idea of leaving you alone in the house with kids I haven't even met."

"We're just going to play board games on the patio. I swear we won't hang out inside. How could we possibly get into any trouble? And I'll clean up afterward and everything. Please?"

Mom gave me a level look. "Do we really embarrass you that much, Chloe?"

"Mom, these are kids I'm going to hang out with a lot over the next year. I don't want them to think I'm a baby who has to be looked after by her mother. I want them to like me."

She didn't look convinced. "And they won't like you if I'm around?"

"Well, no, that's not what I meant. I just don't want what happened in Utah to happen here." We'd lived in Utah before moving to Arizona. While I hadn't been bullied or teased, the kids there had never accepted me, and I spent those two years pretty much keeping to myself. I didn't want to go through that again. "Come on, Mom, please? Can't you go hang out with some of your new friends for a few hours? Maybe the Werners?"

She sighed heavily. "Okay, okay, if it means that much to you. But you stay on the back patio, except to use the bathroom. No one goes to your bedroom, especially not you with a boy." She gave me *that* look, and I colored, remembering how she'd caught me with Sam. "Everyone leaves by nine thirty. And you have all the dishes done and the kitchen cleaned by ten. And please don't burn the house down." She dried her hands then turned to leave. "I'll call Janet."

I jumped up and down. "Thank you, Mom! I promise I won't burn the house down!"

Anna was the first to arrive. She showed up twenty minutes early.

"Hey, girl!" she exclaimed happily as she sauntered into the house. "Anyone else here?"

"Nope. You're the first. Come out back with me."

I led her to the back patio and opened up the cooler. "Drink?"

"Yeah, Pepsi is good, thanks. So I heard you met Hudson and London today."

I passed her a can. "Yeah. At the pool."

"So you got a face full of woman boobs then."

I laughed. "Yeah, you could say that. She's ... "

"An 'early bloomer.'" She made air quotes. "I kind of hate her sometimes," Anna said, taking a drink.

"But she seems really nice," I said.

"Oh, she is. Too nice, sometimes. But don't think she's a push-over. She can be a hard-ass when she needs to be."

We sat side by side at the patio table. "So I noticed ... " I wasn't sure how to ask about this. "She was all bright and bubbly for a while. Then Stacy showed up."

Anna laughed. "And it was like two strange cats

meeting in an alley?"

"Well, sort of. What's going on there?"

"Alex," she said simply.

"Alex?"

"Yeah. Remember how I said that Stacy is obsessed with Alex? She's totally jealous that Alex and London are so close. Last year, when Alex and Callie were broken up, Stacy thought that Alex hooked up with London, and she started a fight with London. They practically tried to kill each other."

Wow. There'd certainly been a lot of drama, way more than I was used to. "Did he?" I asked.

"Did he what?"

"Did Alex hook up with London?"

"Oh. No. At least that's what Alex and London say. I wouldn't be surprised, though, judging by how close the two of them are."

This was making my head spin.

"Okay, wait," I said, putting my hand up. "So Stacy and Alex have been on-and-off again for a long time."

"Yep."

"And they were together for a while his eighth-grade year."

"Yep."

"But then they broke up, and he went out with that girl Callie during his ninth-grade year?"

"That's right," she said.

"And he cheated on her with Stacy."

"That's the general consensus."

"And now you're telling me he might have fooled around with London, too?" I asked incredulously. "While he was also doing stuff with Stacy and Callie?"

"Yep. It's like a soap opera."

It really was. I had this strange sensation in my chest, and it took me a few moments to realize what it was.

Disappointment.

In Alex.

He seemed like such a nice guy, but was he really? I mean, he'd cheated on his girlfriend with another girl, maybe two. Only a scumbag would do that.

I noticed Anna giving me a stern look.

"I know what you're thinking, and you're wrong," she said. "Alex is a good guy. Better than good. He's amazing. What you're not getting is what it's like to live here with just a handful of other kids as your social universe. There's not a lot of options when it comes to who you're going to mess around with. And because you get to know everyone so well it's just easy to slip into that kind of relationship with someone. Don't judge him."

I looked back at her, an eyebrow raised. "You sound like you speak from experience."

She groaned. "Yes. And I wish I could erase some of those experiences. But seriously, don't judge him."

I nodded. "Okay." I guess I could give him a chance.

The doorbell rang then, and I jumped up to go answer it. "I'll be right back."

Hudson, London, and Avery stood there waiting for me. London looked sort of flustered standing next to Avery.

"Hey, guys," I said. "Thanks for coming."

Then I noticed that Alex wasn't with them. "Where's Alex? And Stacy?"

I almost missed it because it was so brief, but a look passed between Hudson and London.

"Not sure," Hudson said. "He wasn't at home when we called. But he said he'd be here. So you said something about burgers?"

"Yeah," I responded. "Come in. We're hanging out on the back patio. The grill is almost ready."

"Are your parents here?" London asked as they stepped into the house.

"No. But they'll be back around ten. I have to kick everyone out at nine thirty, though."

We waited fifteen more minutes, but neither Alex or Stacy showed up. So I got busy grilling the burgers and bringing out the rest of the food and making sure everyone had a soda.

Half an hour later, while we were all eating, there was a knock on the back patio door, and it opened. Alex and Stacy came in, their cheeks rosy and their motions fluid.

"Sorry we're late," Alex said, practically stumbling in. "We were ... uh ... we were—"

"Busy," Stacy interrupted, then burst out laughing. "Really busy." She came over and sat down next to Avery. She whispered something to her and then she giggled. Her eyes were glassed over.

Alex was trying not to smile, but he wasn't doing a very good job at it.

"Oh man," he said with an odd lilt to his voice. "I am so hungry. Did you save us some?"

He stepped close to me, and as he passed I could smell … was that alcohol?

"Hey, Chloe, thanks for—"

I reached out, grabbed him by his arm, and yanked him to the kitchen door. I pulled us both in and shut the door behind us.

"Are you drunk?"

He looked at me with confusion for a few seconds. "Uh … yeah, sort of."

And suddenly I knew what Stacy had meant by "busy." He'd gone out to drink with her and who knows what else. It was ridiculous. Even stupid. But suddenly I was furious.

"What were you thinking?" I demanded. "What if my parents were home?"

"But they're not, right?"

"That's not the point! If they *were* home, they'd able to tell that you're drunk. And then do you know how much trouble I'd be in? They'd kick everyone out. I'd be humiliated."

But that wasn't the real reason I was angry. It was

knowing that he'd been out messing around with Stacy. That hurt.

His eyes were wide. "Hey, whoa. No one's going to get in trouble. I came in through the back patio on purpose so we wouldn't have to meet with your parents at the front door. I wanted to make sure it was cool before making an appearance. I wouldn't have barged in like that if your parents had been around. In fact, I wouldn't have come over at all. I wouldn't want to get you in trouble."

"Oh," was all I could say. So he'd thought this out. He'd had a plan. And he'd thought of me. I guess I shouldn't be all that upset.

But I was.

And it irritated me that I was because I knew it was foolish. I didn't want to be jealous that he'd been with Stacy, or that they'd obviously been messing around. It wasn't as if I had a claim on him—I hadn't even known him for a whole day. And, really, it wasn't any of my business who he fooled around with.

"And we didn't bring any alcohol over," he continued. "I wouldn't do that to you. And we didn't really have that much to drink."

"You smell like a distillery," I told him.

"It's the sadiki," he said. "I told you it's really strong. But food will mask the smell. Trust me. I've been doing this for a while. I know what I'm doing."

"Okay," I replied shortly. "But if my parents show up you and Stacy have to leave."

"Got it," he said.

"Come on." I opened the patio door and waited for him to follow me. "Your burger is probably cold."

As it turned out, and despite the rocky start, we managed to settle in to a nice evening. After they had eaten, neither Alex or Stacy appeared to be drunk anymore, and the smell of alcohol was lost to the aroma of hamburgers. Stacy calmed down, although she and London kept staring daggers at each other—I was a little bit worried that they'd throw down right there on my back patio.

For his part, Alex seemed to ignore them both.

Instead, he focused on me.

Which made me happy.

"Can I help you clean up?" he asked after we'd all finished our meals.

Mom had said not to have anyone in the house, but did having my friends help cleaning up count? I decided it would be okay.

"Sure, thanks. Just bring everything in for me, and I'll do the dishes and put everything away. Then you can set up the Monopoly board. We should play on the ground, though, 'cause there's not enough room on the table."

"Okay."

It took about twenty minutes to get everything cleaned up and all the dishes washed. By that time, the Monopoly board had been set up, and the cash handed out to each player.

"I'm the banker!" Alex declared proudly. "Come sit." He patted the ground next to him.

I felt Stacy's eyes on me, and when I glanced at her, she was looking back at me with her eyes narrowed.

In just a few minutes the game was started. It was quiet at first, but as the game progressed our excitement increased and we began to talk excitedly and laugh. Whenever someone did really well, the rest of us groaned, and when they did particularly badly, we teased them. Alex, who had moved closer to me, acquired several good properties, and it wasn't long before he started winning the game. He wasn't very gracious about it.

"Power! Prestige! Influence!" he would say when someone had to fork over cash to him. "Bwahaha!"

But then Avery got both Boardwalk and Park Place, and she and Alex faced off.

I was enjoying myself, content with my mediocre position, and liking being close to Alex.

I'd kicked off my sandals and sat cross-legged as I played. When I felt something touch my ankle, I absentmindedly brushed at it, but my fingers encountered nothing.

And then, like in a horror movie, something skittered onto the board. It was a spider, bigger than my hand, and had the biggest fangs I'd ever seen.

There was a chorus of screaming and shouting as we attempted to stand and run away at the same time. The spider paused in the middle of the board, then launched itself onto Stacy's lap. Her face turned deathly pale and her scream pierced the night. She swatted at the giant spider, and it landed back on the board. By then, we'd all managed to get to our feet. Avery yanked Stacy up, and we ran out to the backyard, all of us panicked.

"What the hell was that?!" I exclaimed, holding my hand up my chest, feeling my heart pounding underneath.

There was a moment of silence, then Alex burst out laughing. Hudson and London joined in.

Stacy, however, was not amused.

"That wasn't funny!" she shouted, looking like she was about to cry.

Avery stepped up and wrapped her in a hug. "It's okay," she said to Stacy. "Mama is here."

"Seriously," I said, looking at them all in turn. "What was that thing?" My heart was still racing.

"Camel spider," Hudson said.

"Big one, too," Alex added. "Holy shit, that scared the crap out of me."

"That was a spider?" I asked, still feeling scared. "It was huge!"

"Actually," Hudson said, "It's not really a spider. I think it's related to scorpions."

"For crying out loud!" Stacy shouted. "Who cares what it is. It nearly killed me! I am *not* going back over there."

Alex looked around at our feet. "It's probably not

on the patio anymore," he said ominously.

Poor Stacy gasped, and London said, "Oh crap!"

Then we all ran back onto the patio, through the kitchen door, and inside my house.

A nervous laugh escaped me. "Holy bananas! Are those things common here?"

"You see them from time to time," Anna said. "But they're usually not that big. That might have been the biggest one I've ever seen."

"I've seen bigger," Hudson said.

Why? Why did my parents have to move me to a desert where giant man-eating spiders lived? Or Scorpions. Or whatever the hell it was.

"I am way too freaked to go back out there," London said. "Can we stay in here, Chloe? Please?"

Mom specifically said not to hang out in the house. But then again, that camel spider was a game changer. If I explained to Mom what had happened, and described the spider in detail, maybe she would understand.

"Okay," I said. "We can maybe watch something on TV."

We made our way into the living room, and everyone found a place either on the sofa, a chair or the floor. I watched, irritated, as Stacy sat next to Alex, angling her body so that her legs draped over his.

I sat on the floor with Hudson.

We settled in to watch the second half of *Trading Places* on CCTV, and then, as promised, I made everyone leave at nine thirty.

We said goodbye and agreed to meet at the pool the following day.

With some trepidation, I went out to the patio to pick up the game board and all the pieces, hoping like crazy that the giant spider had made its way somewhere far, far away.

The next day, Anna, Stacy, and A
made small talk with them, but
making faces, begging her to stop.

Alex, Hudson, and London
pool, laying out on lounge cha
different bikini which seemed to
red one had just barely , but he
display, and her abundant chest w

Again, I felt inadequate and
did my best to hide it.

About a half hour later, I
Hudson reached into a bag he'd
out what appeared to be a LEGO

Alex had one, too.

I smiled. So they were still like

"What are those?" I asked.

"Submarines," Alex said, as
creation.

"'They look like spaceships," I replied. "What are you going to do with them?"

"Hudson and I have this competition going. We build these subs and let them loose in the deep end of the pool. 'The ship that takes the longest to reach the bottom wins. 'The winner gets bragging rights."

"'They've been doing this forever," Anna said from her chaise where she lay, sunglasses covering her eyes.

"Is that why they have wings?"

"Yeah," Alex answered. "So they kind of glide to the bottom." He stood and looked to Hudson. "Ready to be embarrassed?"

"Ready to be embarrassed for you," Hudson replied, then stood.

'The two of them walked over to the edge of the pool and carefully got in, holding their LEGO creations. 'They paddled to the center of the deep end then submerged themselves.

"'They're like little kids," I said to no one in particular.

"Alex sure wasn't like a little kid last night," Stacy said.

Anna and I looked at each other, and she rolled her eyes.

What was Stacy's deal? Why did she need to remind everyone that she and Alex had been together last night? Was she trying to rub it in London's face? Or was she just staking her claim on him?

I looked to London who was still laying on her

back, seemingly unaffected by Stacy's words.

I couldn't say the same, though. I was irritated. And jealous. And sort of amazed.

Had Stacy and Alex just been kissing and stuff? Or had they had sex? Is that what Anna had meant by Stacy being experienced?

I couldn't quite believe it. Stacy was only fourteen. That was way too young to be having sex. I mean, I certainly hadn't been doing anything like that. Sam had been my first and only boyfriend, and the farthest we'd gone was his hand on my boob over my shirt. And none of my friends back home had done anything more than that, either.

But the kids here ... they seemed to be very mature for their age. They drank. They fooled around with each other. Maybe even had sex. And they acted like it was normal.

"Going in," Stacy said, and she and Avery got up and dove into the deep end. They swam to be near the boys but kept a small distance as they paddled water and talked.

"Want to go in?" I asked Anna.

"Yep." Anna scooped up the volleyball she'd brought. "London?"

"Okay, sure."

That was how things were for the next two days. We spent the day at the pool, and at night we hung out on the bleachers by the softball field. There really wasn't anything else to do. I was beginning to understand what Alex had meant about it being boring here.

But hanging out, not doing much of anything, was good enough.

The third evening, as the girls were hanging out on the bleachers, Alex and Hudson showed up with a guy I didn't know.

The three of them walked over, each one carrying a large bottle of Mirinda, an orange soda.

London jumped up and hurried over to the boys and gave the newcomer a hug. It was quick, not like the hug she'd given Alex, but it was clear London knew the new boy pretty well.

They all came over and sat with us. The new guy was about the same height as Alex and Hudson, but he was more heavily built, kind of stocky, and strong looking—his waist was thick, his shoulders were wide, and the muscles of his arms stretched the fabric of his T-shirt. His dark hair was straight, and his bangs covered his eyes, just like Alex's, but his hair was longer. He wasn't particularly cute—I had to admit the muscles were kind of sexy, though—but he had a gentleness about him that was endearing.

Anna came over to give the new arrival a hug, but Stacy and Avery remained sitting and just said hi.

Alex gestured to me. "That's Chloe," he told the

new kid. "She's new. Chloe, this is Logan."

"Hey, Chloe," Logan said, giving me a wave.

I waved back. "Hi, Logan. Nice to meet you."

The boys sat with us, and each one unscrewed the cap of their bottles and offered them to the girls. Only Avery refrained. They each took a drink and then made a scrunched up face.

Alex looked over to me when London handed the bottle back to him. "If you want some just ask, okay?"

Oh

"Is that ... "

"Sadiki and Mirinda," he replied. "It tastes like shit, but it packs a punch."

Were they all going to get drunk? Would I be the only loser not drinking? No. Avery hadn't had any. But London and Anna and Stacy had, and they acted like it was no big deal.

"Um ... no, I'm good," I said.

Alex smiled at me. "It's okay if you don't want any," he said reassuringly. "We won't push you."

There was a lot of excited chatter as everyone asked Logan about his summer. Logan, apparently, was a bit of an adventurer. He had spent his summer going from one national park to another, camping and hiking with his brother and sister, both of whom were a lot older than he was.

Logan had a quiet way about him, and I found myself calmed by his smooth, gentle voice. There was something about him that put me at ease and made me feel like I could trust him.

"What are you guys going to do?" London asked once it was clear Logan had run out of stories. She had one of the bottles and took a drink, making a grimace afterward.

"We were thinking of going over the wall to the club," Hudson said. "You girls want to come?"

The club?

"Sure," London answered, and Stacy and Avery both nodded.

"What's the club?" I asked, somewhat nervous. Did I want to go somewhere with them where they would be drinking?

"It's kind of a fort the boys built," Anna said. "It's over the wall, next to the dry river bed, by the trees. We hang out there sometimes. It's pretty neat. You'll like it."

"Over the wall?" I was still nervous. "Like out in the desert?"

"Yeah," she replied. "We go over all the time. It's not a big deal."

This was making me a bit uncomfortable. But if everyone went, I'd be left alone, and look like a total loser.

No one was pushing me to do this, but I still felt pressured. What if we were caught? My parents would lose their minds if they found out I went over the wall to hang out with kids who were drinking.

Crap

"Okay," I said.

"Good," Alex said. "It'll be fun."

We all stood and followed the boys towards the housing area. They led us down the street next to the southernmost wall, toward Anna's house, then stepped between two houses to get to the wall behind. There were no lights, so it was dark.

When we reached the wall, the boys handed their bottles to London and Stacy. The wall was about eight feet high, but that wasn't an obstacle for the boys. The three of them jumped up, grabbed the top and pulled themselves up. Alex and Hudson straddled the wall, facing each other, and Logan slipped over the edge to the other side. The girls handed the bottles to Alex and Hudson and they, in turn, tossed them down to Logan on the other side.

There was a system. It was clear they'd done this before.

London walked up to the wall, and Alex and Hudson reached down. She jumped, and the boys latched on to her wrists and pulled her up. Then she threw both legs over the wall and lowered herself down the other side where I presumed Logan was there to catch her.

Stacy, Avery, and Anna repeated the procedure and made it over the wall.

Then it was my turn.

I mimicked what I'd seen the other girls do. I jumped up with my arms stretched out over me, and

Alex and Hudson pulled me up.

"You okay?" Alex asked as I swung my legs over.

"Yeah. Fine."

Then I lowered myself down the other side of the wall until I was hanging by my hands. I felt Logan grab my hips.

"I got you," he said, and I let go with a tiny yelp.

Logan was as strong as he looked. He lowered me gently down until my feet touched the ground.

"You okay?" he asked, just like Alex had.

"Yeah, I'm fine. Thanks."

It was really dark.

London must have read my mind because she said, "It takes a little while to get used to the dark. We'll just wait here for a bit."

Alex and Hudson lowered themselves to the ground. I could barely make them out in the darkness.

The sky was clear, and a half-moon hung low in the west. Eventually, with the help of the faraway lights of the softball field, our eyes got used to the dark.

"Okay," Alex said. "Let's go."

The girls followed the boys as we walked out into the desert. I was still nervous, but also a little bit excited. I was doing something *bad,* and I kind of liked the rush it was giving me.

And I felt like I was becoming one of them. Like I was being initiated into their club or something.

We didn't say anything as we walked.

It didn't take long before I was able to make out

where we were going. Up ahead was a copse of trees. It was too dark to make out how many. As we got closer, I could see that there were also bushes and smaller trees that made a sort of wall around a central, large tree with their foliage.

The boys dropped down a small, sandy embankment and then turned around to help the girls down. I guessed this was the dry river bed.

And then a totally surprising thing happened.

Alex came close and grabbed my hand, then laced his fingers together with mine. "Stay close," he said. "It's kind of sandy."

I tightened my grip on his hand as a different kind of thrill ran through me. "Okay."

We approached an opening in the trees and stepped into a leafy cave of sorts. The walls were just the smaller trees and bushes that surrounded the big tree in the center, and the canopy above us provided sparse cover.

Alex let go of my hand, and then suddenly there was a light, and I realized Hudson had turned on a flashlight.

I was sort of irritated.

"Why didn't you use that sooner?" I asked.

"Because someone might have noticed it," Alex explained. "And sometimes the security guards do a circuit around the walls. They'd see a flashlight for sure."

"Oh." Wow. They had all this stuff down to a

science.

"But it's okay in here?" I asked, feeling like we were going to be caught at any second.

"Yeah, it's good. The trees and the embankment provide cover."

From somewhere—I didn't know where—Alex and Logan produced flashlights of their own.

With the new light, I was able to take in my surroundings. We stood in a small clearing, maybe twenty feet wide, at the base of the largest tree. Wood boards had been placed against the smaller trees and bushes to make crude walls. In the center of the clearing was a fire pit, which looked like it hadn't been used in a long time. And around it sat four beat-up folding chairs and two logs.

"I'll get some wood," Logan said, then disappeared outside.

"We're going to start a fire?" I asked, feeling alarmed again.

"Relax, Chloe," Alex said. "We do this all the time. Have a seat."

The girls each took a seat on the chairs and logs, while the boys waited for Logan to return.

Soon enough, Logan stepped into the clearing, his arms loaded up with branches. "There's more," he said, and Alex and Hudson stepped out, only to return with smaller bundles of wood.

They all dumped the branches on the sand next to the fire pit, and Logan knelt down and started arranging the smaller branches in a neat pile.

Anna must have read the question on my face because she leaned in. "Boy Scout," she said in explanation.

It didn't take Logan long to start a small fire. When he was satisfied, he scooted away from the pit and crossed his legs. Hudson and Alex did the same.

Then they started passing the bottles around. Avery and I didn't have any, but everyone else did. Avery didn't seem to be self-conscious about not drinking, and that made me feel better. I guess if you didn't want to drink the others wouldn't try to push you into it.

As they drank, they began to talk about their summer vacations, quietly at first, but louder and louder the more they drank. Mostly it was the boys and London talking because they'd been away. Stacy, Avery, and Anna had all stayed in Taif the entire summer, so they didn't have a lot to contribute.

It wasn't long before their speech became a little slurred and they swayed in their seats. Stacy had moved to the ground next to Alex, and she laid herself out and put her head on his lap. London noticed this, but she didn't seem to care. She'd started up a separate conversation with Anna and Logan about the boarding school she was going to attend.

Then Alex did something surprising.

"Hey, Chloe!" he called a little louder than was necessary. "Tell us about Arizona."

"Arizona?"

"Yeah. Like your school and your friends and stuff you did."

"Um ... but it's all so boring."

He laughed at that. "Not to us. We only visit the States about once a year. We have no idea what it's like to live there. You know ... go to school there and stuff. Tell us about it."

Had he noticed I'd just been sitting quietly as they talked? Was he trying to include me? Make me feel part of the group?

Was he thinking of me that much?

That thought made a warm, fluttery feeling settle in my chest, and I couldn't help but blush.

So I began to talk.

I told them about Glendale. About my friends, the school I went to, my swim club and reading group. They asked questions about the things I'd done with my friends, about going to movies and hanging out at the mall. They wanted to know all about stuff that I thought would bore them, but they all seemed interested. Ironically, the way I'd grown up—what I considered boring and normal—was something exotic to them.

Eventually, I ran out of things to say.

"I have to go back," Anna said after a few moments of silence. "I have to check in."

"Yeah, okay," Alex said. "Let's go."

Going back was more of an adventure because they

were all a bit drunk. They stumbled along in the dark and kept talking in loud voices. I was worried that the boys wouldn't be able to get us over the wall, but it wasn't a problem. It took more time, but they repeated the process and got all the girls over.

We split up then. When I saw Alex and Stacy had paired up, that same painful jealousy rose up inside of me. The two of them said goodbye and walked off, probably to go somewhere to make out. Or worse.

Anna, Avery and I left together since we all had to check in at home, and we left London, Hudson and Logan behind.

It had been an interesting evening, and even though I hadn't had anything to drink, I felt like I was becoming part of the group. And I knew that the way Alex had made sure to make me a focus of conversation had a lot to do with that.

Alex was so confusing. He seemed to like me. He went out of his way to make sure I was included. He didn't pressure me into doing anything I wasn't comfortable with. He didn't judge me. And he was gentle with me.

But what was the deal with him and Stacy? Were they going out? Or did they just have a casual thing going on? And why did it bother me so much?

Well, okay, that was a dumb question. I knew why it bothered me. I was just having a hard time admitting it myself. But I couldn't deny it. What Alex and Stacy were doing bothered me because I was jealous. I wanted Alex to take me off somewhere to make out. I wanted him to pay me the same kind of attention he did to Stacy.

And then there was London.

She was really nice, and I liked her even though I kind of hated her for making me feel like I was as flat as an ironing board . She had such a casual familiarity with Alex that it made me wonder about their relationship, especially with Stacy thrown into the mix. London acted as if she knew that what she had with Alex was beyond his relationship with Stacy. Like she wasn't bothered that the two of them messed around because she knew that what she shared with Alex was something Stacy could never have.

And that bothered me, too.

I wanted what both of them had with Alex. I wanted him for myself.

But I knew I never would. He would be leaving for boarding school soon, and then who knew if and when I would ever see him again. That left just a few days to spend time with him. But how could I compete with Stacy or London who had been with him for years?

The days played out with increasing familiarity. I got up, had breakfast, then went to the pool where the rest of my new friends would gather.

Anna and I were usually the first to arrive at the pool, but sometimes Stacy and Avery were there before us. London sometimes arrived on her own, but usually, she came with the boys, who always seemed to be together.

Sometimes, it was clear that they'd been drinking the night before because they were a bit subdued when they arrived, and their eyes were red. But it didn't take them long to recover. After drinking lots of water and just hanging out, the life returned to them and soon they were goofing off and laughing with each other.

I found it really weird how, during the day, Alex and Stacy kept a distance between themselves. Alex mostly interacted with Hudson, Logan, and London, which seemed to annoy Stacy, judging by the way she would look over at them with her eyes narrowed.

There was another interesting thing to watch.

London was very friendly with Hudson and Logan. She would do things like put her hand on their arms or shoulders when they made her laugh. In the pool, she would get into splash fights with them and laugh and squeal when they ganged up on her. It was easy to see that they were good friends that had spent a lot of time with each other.

But she was different with Alex. London didn't seem to go out of her way to be close to him—at least that's how it looked to me—but if they were together she looked at him like he was the single most important person in her world. She was generally upbeat and happy, but she really glowed when she was with Alex.

At first, I assumed she was in love with him, but

the more I watched them together, the more I began to doubt that. It was obvious that they were close in a way they weren't with anyone else, but I didn't think their feelings were romantic. There just wasn't a spark between them, no sexual tension at all. Nothing like that. They were just two people who seemed to care deeply for each other.

When we'd had enough of the sun and the pool, we'd all go home to check in with our parents and have something to eat, and maybe have a nap.

Then we would meet up again in the evening, usually at the bleachers, and hang out. The boys would sometimes bring alcohol, and London and Stacy would have some—sometimes Anna did too—but Avery and I refrained. We would stay at the bleachers or move to the playground, but we didn't do anything beyond just spending time with each other, talking and laughing.

Even though there wasn't much to do, I was having fun. And every day, more and more, I felt like I belonged. And I began to understand what Anna had said about having just a small handful of kids be your entire social world.

In just a few days, I realized I'd made friends who seemed closer to me than any I'd ever had before.

There was something magical about that.

CHAPTER SEVEN

A few days later, after I ate breakfast and was about to head to the pool, there was a knock at the door.

I ran to open it, expecting Anna, but instead, Alex was standing there, a board game tucked under his arm.

"Hi," he said with a brilliant smile that made me all fluttery.

"Hi," I said back, trying not to grin like an idiot. "Are we going to the pool? Where's Anna?"

He rubbed the back of his head with his free hand and gave me that lopsided grin I loved so much. "Well, I was hoping we could do something just the two of us."

Oh my gosh

"Really? Like what?"

"I brought a game. Can I come in?"

"Oh, geez, I'm so sorry. Come in."

We stepped into the house just as Mom came out to see who had knocked on the door.

"Oh! Alex. So nice to see you again. How are you?"

"I'm fine, thanks," he answered. "How are you, Mrs. Parker?"

"Just fine," she said, then beamed at him. "Are you headed off to the pool?"

"No, ma'am. I brought a game over to play with Chloe."

Mom's face did this little jump thing she did whenever she realized something unexpected, and she looked between Alex and me a few times like she was puzzling something out.

"Oh," she finally said, satisfied with whatever conclusion she'd come to. "How nice."

I could tell she was about to say something embarrassing, so I butted in and boldly grabbed Alex's hand. "We're going to hang out in my room," I blurted out.

Mom opened her mouth to speak, but I beat her to it.

"I know. Door stays open." As much as she seemed to like Alex, she still didn't want us making out and fondling each other in my room. Just thinking about it made me blush.

When we were in my room—with the door open—I turned to Alex. "I'm sorry about her. I wish she wouldn't mention the door thing like she suspects we're going to ... you know."

Alex laughed. "Don't worry about it. She's just trying to be a good mom. So I brought this board game

73

I thought you'd like." He held it out to me, and I took it from him.

It was called Dungeon and had cool fantasy art all over the box. "Hey, that's neat," I said, and I sat on my bed. "I've never heard of this."

Alex sat next to me. "Do you want to play? It's easy to learn."

He had no idea how much I wanted to spend time alone with him. And even more so because I knew he'd been thinking of me and wanted to be alone with me, too. It made me almost giddy.

"I'd love to," I said.

"Okay, great. On the floor or on the bed?"

I wondered what Mom would think about Alex and me being together on my bed. I decided to risk it. "On the bed," I said, blushing like crazy.

"Okay, let's get it set up."

In just a few minutes we were playing the game. It was pretty simple, and I picked up the rules quickly. We didn't engage in any meaningful conversation, just talked about the game as we played, and even though I was enjoying being with him, I was a little bit disappointed that we weren't really talking.

Then he got really quiet. He looked behind him like he was making sure my mom wasn't lurking in the doorway, then he spoke. "Hey, I wanted to ask you something. Or, actually just talk about it, I guess."

I nodded.

He looked down at the game board. "I sort of get

this feeling that you really don't like that we drink alcohol. I feel like you're disappointed in me." He looked up at me, and his eyes were shy.

My heart skipped a beat, as I realized what he was really saying. He cared what I thought of him.

He was thinking of me again.

A pleasant warmth hummed inside me.

"No," I said, my voice low. "It's not that. It's just that I'm not used to it. My friends and I never did anything like that back home. We wouldn't even have known where to start. I've always thought that drinking was what older teenagers did, you know? Keg parties and all that? I never expected you all would be so casual about drinking at our age."

He looked past my shoulder and pursed his lips as he considered my words. "I guess you'd have to have lived here as long as us to understand. There's nothing to do here. I think you're beginning to see that. And we get really bored. And, you know, it's so easy to get alcohol here. Sometimes it seems like it just falls onto our laps. So we drink. I've just always done it. But it doesn't mean I'm a bad person."

His voice was so tender, it tugged at my heart. "I don't think you're a bad person, Alex. I just think we grew up very differently."

"Are you sure?" he asked.

I wanted to say, "Not about you and Stacy." I was still troubled by his casual sexual relationship with her. Maybe I was a prude, but I felt that you shouldn't be doing stuff like that with someone unless you were together with them. To just do it casually didn't sit that well with me.

But I didn't want to judge him, so I just said, "Yes, I'm sure."

"Okay, good," he said, looking relieved. "I was kind of worried."

I was touched again by how much he seemed to care what I thought of him.

"Hey," he said, sounding like his usual self. "Let's play a couple of rounds, and then will you show me more of your art?"

And there it was again. He was interested in me.

I got all fluttery inside.

"Sure," I said. "I think I'd like that."

We played the game twice, and I beat him both times. He was cute when he pouted.

After we'd put the game away, I stood and walked over to my desk. I opened the top drawer and pulled out my folder that contained all of the drawings I'd been working on over the past six months.

Suddenly it felt as if I were about to do something important, something meaningful, intimate even.

With my back to him, I took a deep breath, and let it out.

I turned around and sat back on the bed, my gaze cast down. Did I really want to do this?

"Are you okay?" he asked.

"Yeah. It's just ... I guess I'm nervous. Which is

ridiculous. Back home I had my drawings taped up on my walls, and anyone who came over could see them. But ... "

He reached over and touched my arm. "But now it feels personal? Like you're sharing something private?"

My head snapped up and I looked at him with surprise. He'd read my mind.

"Yes," I said. "That's exactly it."

"I understand, you know. I feel that way about my writing. You don't have to show me. I get it."

"I want to." But I didn't just want to do this casually. I wanted to show him each drawing one by one, explain what they meant to me, why I'd drawn them. I wanted him to see beyond what was visible. I wanted him to see me.

"Okay," he said. "Show me."

So I laid the folder down on the bed between us.

"This is me," I said.

I opened the folder and began to show him my art.

Alex listened carefully, never interrupting, as I explained each drawing. He took each one and studied it, noticing every detail.

That made me smile. He wanted to know something personal about me. Once again, he was showing an interest in me, in who I was. He wanted to know me better.

It took almost an hour to go through all of the drawings.

"Thank you," he said, smiling as he looked at me.

"For showing me your work. I wish I was as brave as you. I could never let anyone read my stuff. I'm scared to put myself out there like you just did."

"It's okay," I said. "I understand."

"Chloe!" Mom called out from down the hall. "Anna is here!"

A few seconds later, Anna stepped into my room.

"Hey, girl! I was—" Then she saw Alex. "Oh, hey Alex. I thought you were at the pool."

"Nope," he said. "Chloe and I were playing a game." He held up the box.

Anna looked between us a few times, and I could almost see the gears turning in her head. Then she smiled. "Well, everyone is at the pool," she said. "You guys want to come?"

Alex stood up and walked to the door. "Yeah, sounds good. I have to go home and change, so I'll see you guys there." He looked back at me. "See you in a bit."

After he left, Anna rushed over, a grin on her face.

"How long was he here?" she asked.

"About two hours," I said, feeling shy again for some reason.

"And you guys were alone the whole time?"

"Yes."

"Huh."

"What?" I asked. "Is there something weird about that?"

"No. It's just that ... never mind. Hurry up and get

changed. I'll wait for you up front."

When we arrived at the pool, we found everyone sitting at the picnic tables under the pavilion having lunch. After Anna and I got our own food, we joined them.

Alex sat in the middle of a bench with Hudson and London on either side of him. London, of course, was close to him, their hips touching. I looked over to the next table where Stacy and Avery were sitting to gauge Stacy's reaction, but her attention was on Avery as they talked about something.

Anna and I sat next to Logan, and ate in silence while everyone continued a conversation about something called "316."

"It's still empty," Alex said. "Hudson and I checked it out last night."

"You guys sneaked out?" London asked as she finished off her French fries.

"Yeah," Hudson replied. "We wanted to see if it was still empty."

"What are you guys talking about?" I asked. "What's 316?"

"It's an empty house in camp two," Hudson said. "It's been empty for over a year. No one lives there."

"We used to hang out there and drink when we would sneak out at night," Alex said.

"You guys broke into an empty house?" I asked,

not quite surprised about this new revelation.

"Well, no, not really," Alex said, grinning. "The patio door was unlocked the first time we were there, so we didn't actually have to break anything."

"And you guys sneak out in the middle of the night and go drink there?"

"Sometimes," London said. "It's usually only the boys. I've only been there a few times. I don't like to sneak out at night."

"I've never been there," Anna piped in. "I'm not brave enough to sneak out at night. But Stacy's been there plenty of times."

That didn't surprise me either. Of all the girls, Stacy seemed to be the one that engaged in illicit activities with the boys. I guessed that was because of Alex.

"Are you guys going tonight?" I asked.

"We were thinking about it," Hudson said. "We sort of wanted to hang out there one last time before we have to leave for boarding school. Do you want to come with us?"

My eyes widened. "Sneak out at night? No way. I'd be grounded until I'm sixty if my parents caught me."

"Hey, don't worry about it," Alex said. "I don't think I want to go either." He caught my eye and gave me a wink. "I need my beauty sleep."

And there it was again. He didn't want me to feel left out. He didn't want me to feel pressured. I was *so* thankful for his consideration.

Anna barked out a laugh but didn't say anything.

"Yeah, it's kind of dumb." Logan broke his silence. "I don't think I want to get in trouble this close to leaving for boarding school."

"I guess," Hudson said. "That makes sense."

I hadn't noticed before, but I realized Alex was the leader of this group. He dictated what they did and didn't do. They turned to him for guidance. Now that I thought about it, it was obvious. And not all that surprising. Alex was very charismatic. He had this way about him that commanded attention, that made you want to follow him. It was in his eyes. There was a promise of adventure in them, a spark of life, something ... something that I was ...

Oh my gosh I'm falling in love with him

Of course, this had to happen. Of course, I had to fall in love with a boy who would leave my life in just a few days. I wasn't going to get a chance to see if we could be more than friends. It wasn't fair. I didn't want him to leave. I didn't want to lose him.

Anna stood up, grabbed my arm and pulled me up. "We'll be right back," she said to everyone else.

She dragged me off to the farthest picnic table over by the kiddie pool.

"What's wrong?" she asked after we sat down together, concern on her face. "Why are you crying?"

hat?

I reached up to my face to feel it wet with tears.

Anna sat me down on the bench and settled in next

to me. "You got all quiet. And then you were crying. What happened?"

"I ... " I didn't know what to say.

Anna studied me, her eyes probing my face. Then she closed her eyes for a few seconds and shook her head slightly. "Holy crap."

"I ... I think I'm in love with Alex." I felt more tears run down my face.

"Holy crap," she said again, and reached out with her arm, putting it around my shoulder and drawing me close to her. "You know he's leaving in three days, right?"

I nodded. Alex and Hudson were leaving first, then London the day after, and finally Logan the day after that.

Anna squeezed me tight. "He won't be back until next summer," she said. "He's going to the Norway for winter break, then somewhere in Asia for his spring break."

"How do you know that?"

"It's not a secret. His parents told me when I was over one day." She squeezed me again. "I'm sorry, Chloe."

I shrugged, pulling away from her and wiping my tears. "It's okay. Even if he were staying, it's not like we could be together. There's Stacy and London. Stacy's been with him forever. And there's no way I could compete with London. It's probably for the best that he's leaving."

Anna pursed her lips. "I'm sorry," she said again. "This has to be hard for you."

I made a little laugh. "I'll get over it. It just took me by surprise when I figured it out."

"Well, if you want to talk about it, I'm here."

"Thanks. I need to go wash my face."

"Do you want to leave?" she asked, still looking concerned. "We can hang out at my place. Watch a movie or something."

"No. It's fine." I did my best to smile. "I want to stay."

Anna understood. She knew I wanted to spend as much time with Alex as I could, to enjoy what little time I had left with him.

"I'll go with you," she said, standing.

"Thanks, Anna. You're a really good friend."

CHAPTER EIGHT

As the day progressed, I began to wonder if Alex knew how I felt. He stayed by me the whole day. He laid out next to me on the lounge chairs, and when I wanted to get in the water, he came in with me. Of course, London, Hudson, and Logan came with us, but they followed his lead. Anna came too, but she stayed with London. Hudson and Logan paired off, taking turns diving and jumping into the pool, trying to outdo each other. That left Alex and me.

London didn't seem bothered by this—she remained calm and casual—but Stacy was a different story. I could feel her eyes on me all day, and not in a good way. But she kept quiet, and she kept her distance just like she had every day we were at the pool.

That was something I just couldn't figure out.

But I was happy to be with Alex, and I did my best not to think about him leaving in a couple of days.

I'd fallen asleep on my lounge chair, and when I

was awakened by the scraping of a chair, I found I was alone with London. She squatted by her chaise, rummaging through her bag.

"Sorry," she said. "I didn't mean to wake you so rudely."

"It's okay. I didn't mean to fall asleep." I sat up and looked around. "Where is everyone?"

"In the snack bar," she said as she continued to root through her bag.

I didn't notice Avery until she was right by us. When Avery's shadow fell across London, London looked up. Then she practically jumped in her haste to stand.

"Avery. Hi."

"Hi. Hey, do you think I can borrow some money? I forgot to bring any."

"Yes! Of course! Here, just let me—" London fumbled with her wallet, but it slipped from her hands and fell to the ground, sending her change rolling in all directions. London blushed crimson as she squatted back down to collect the money. Then she popped back up and faced Avery. "Um, yeah ... how much did you ... I mean ..." She held out her change and bills. "Is this enough?"

Avery, who had been watching with her usual flat expression, cracked a smile. "I'll just take this ten," she said and plucked a bill from London's hand. "Thanks. I'll pay you back tonight." And she walked away.

London watched her go and let out a pathetic sigh. I barely heard her mutter, "Real smooth, London. Real smooth."

That night, after we'd gone home to eat and rest, we met at the bleachers again. The boys had their bottles of sadiki and Mirinda, which they shared with London, Stacy, and Anna, and soon they were a little bit drunk. I was nervous because they talked and laughed loudly. What if an adult came over and demanded to know what was in the bottles? But even though there were plenty of adults who came in and out of the snack bar, not ten yards away, no one seemed to notice us.

"Hey, it's Ryan and Matt!" Anna said excitedly, pointing toward the snack bar. We all turned to look.

Walking toward us were two boys, one my age and the other younger. They both grinned when they saw us watching them. Anna stood and ran to them, giving the older boy a hug, and putting her hand on the younger kid's shoulder.

They walked over to us and took seats as everyone welcomed them.

Anna introduced us. "Chloe, this is Ryan." She gestured to the older boy. "And this is his little brother, Matt. Ryan's in our grade and Matt will be in seventh grade. They've been away for a couple of months."

She then spoke to the boys. "This is Chloe. She's new. She'll be in our grade."

"Hi, Chloe," Ryan said. He was cute in a dorky

sort of way. His brown hair was a little bit messy, and his wire-rimmed glasses perched on his button nose. "Nice to meet you."

Matt's hair was lighter than Ryan's, and he didn't wear glasses. Unlike his brother, he had a scattering of freckles across his nose and cheeks. I could tell he would be a good-looking boy when he got older.

"Hi," I said to them. "Nice to meet you, too."

As we continued talking, I noticed that no one offered Ryan or Matt alcohol.

Matt sat close to London, and it was cute to see that he was totally smitten by her. There was a clear adoration on his face whenever she spoke to him.

I found myself sitting with Anna as Ryan told us about his trip to India and Nepal. As he talked, I could see that he was more than a little bit nerdy. I didn't mind, though, since I considered myself a bit of a geek, too. It was just a contrast to Alex, Hudson, and Logan, who seemed to be so much older than Ryan, even though only a year separated them.

I also noticed that Ryan looked at me more than he did at Anna, and when our eyes met, he blushed, the pink contrasting against his light skin. When I glanced at him, he'd quickly look away.

Then he started asking me questions, and I repeated the things I'd told everyone else when we'd been at the club. He listened attentively, but he'd flit his eyes away from mine whenever our gazes lingered for too long.

It didn't take me long to guess that he had a crush on me.

I didn't know what to think about that.

I was a little bit flattered, but mostly it made me uncomfortable. It wasn't that I found his attention unwelcome. It was just that thinking of Ryan in that way made me feel a little bit like I was cheating on Alex. I didn't like thinking romantic things about another boy when I was in love with Alex.

I hoped that Ryan wouldn't act on his crush.

If that's what it was.

At one point, London passed a bottle to Anna, who took it and had a sip. She then handed the bottle off to Hudson.

I turned to Ryan. "You don't drink?"

"No way," he said. "My parents would completely lose it if they found out."

"Yeah, me too," I said. "I don't drink either."

Ryan looked at me intently for a few seconds. "Good. Sometimes I feel totally left out. But everyone's cool about it. They don't pressure me."

"Same here," I said. "They're nice about it."

"So how are you liking it here?"

"Well, it's a little bit boring."

He grinned. "Yeah. But it gets better once school starts. You'll see. So you mentioned you like to read fantasy."

I nodded. "I do."

"Have you ever heard of Dungeons and Dragons?"

"Yes, but I don't know anything about it."

"Well, I run games sometimes. You should play with us. If you're into fantasy, I think you'd like it. And it's something to do."

That seemed like a good thing. I expected that finding fun things to do would be a challenge.

"Yeah, okay," I said. "I'll give it a go."

He smiled broadly. "Great! We'll probably start a couple of weeks after school starts. Let me tell you how the game works."

And that's how I sat alone with Ryan for over an hour as he explained about his hobby.

Eventually, it got late.

"I have to go," I said to him. "I have a curfew."

"Oh crap," he said, looking at his watch. "Me too. Matt! Time to go."

Matt still had the goofy look on his face, like he'd been in the presence of a divine being. "Okay."

"Will you be at the pool tomorrow?" Ryan asked.

"Probably," I replied.

"Great. I'll be there too. What house are you in?"

"42/."

"Oh, hey! I'm just one street over. Can I walk you home?"

"Sure," I said, feeling uncomfortable with his attention. I hoped that Ryan wouldn't try to kiss me or anything like that. He was sweet, and I didn't want to hurt him by rejecting him.

All of the ninth graders—except for Stacy—split

off to go home. The older kids didn't seem to have a curfew, so they stayed behind.

Alex caught my attention as I made my way down the bleachers, passing by him.

"Hey, can I come over tomorrow?" he asked. "To get you, I mean?"

"Yes, I'd like that," I said, feeling all sorts of happy that he wanted to be with me. "See you tomorrow."

The following two days passed lazily by. Like usual, we spent the late morning and early afternoon hanging out at the pool. But instead of just Alex paying attention to me, I had to handle Ryan as well. On the one hand, Alex stayed close to me, and I was happy about that, but Ryan would come over and talk to me when Alex became distracted with someone else.

My suspicion about Ryan having a crush on me became a certainty. I could tell he was trying to hide it, but the way he got really shy when we talked, and the way he looked at me made it pretty obvious.

Anna noticed, too.

On the second day, when we were eating snacks at the picnic tables, Anna took me aside and sat alone with me.

"So?" she said, a toothy grin on her face.

"So what?" I asked, grabbing some fries and dipping them in ketchup.

"Don't pretend you don't know that Ryan has a

huge crush on you. He's not being very subtle about it. Though the way he thinks he is, is kind of cute."

"Yeah, I noticed," I said.

"And?"

"And what?"

She rolled her eyes. "How do you feel about that?"

I raised one shoulder, let it fall. "I don't know. Flattered I guess? But I'm not interested."

"I figured," she said, stealing one of my fries. "You only have eyes for Alex." We sat in silence for a few moments. "He leaves tomorrow."

"I know."

"Are you ready for that?"

"Would it matter if I was or wasn't? He's leaving either way." My eyes began to sting, but I blinked the tears away.

"Wow," Anna said, coming over to sit by me. She put her arm around me and pulled me against her. "You really are in love with him, aren't you?"

"Yeah. I am. And I'm going to lose him."

She squeezed me again. "I'm sorry."

She didn't say anything else, knowing any further words would be pointless.

The next day, we went to Alex's house to see him and Hudson off. We were all there. We sat in his living room as his dad busied himself with getting Alex's paperwork ready.

After sitting around awkwardly listening to the older kids talk about what they expected boarding school to be like, and the rest of us just nodding sadly, Alex and Hudson stood.

"I better go," Hudson said.

London hugged him and gave him a kiss on the cheek, and he and Logan shared a brief, but emotional hug.

"See you winter break, dude," Logan said to him. "I'll write you."

"Yeah, me too."

The rest of us said goodbye to Hudson, then we all turned to look at Alex.

Logan gave him a brotherly hug. "Gonna miss you, man."

"Yeah," Alex said quietly. "Me too."

Then Anna stepped in and also gave him a hug. "See you next summer."

London hung back as the rest said their goodbyes.

That's when I noticed that tears were streaming down her face, and her lips trembled as she struggled to contain herself. She threw herself at Alex, and they wrapped their arms around each other. Alex buried his face in her hair, looking pained.

Then London stepped back and smiled at him through her tears. "You take care of yourself, okay?"

Alex nodded to her. "Okay."

"And don't forget me."

"Never."

She took in a deep breath and let it out in a shaky rush. "You're my best friend, Alex. I love you."

He looked back at her tenderly. "I love you too, London. Always."

"Okay," she said, stepping back. "Be good." Then she turned, and with a sob ran out the door.

Anna followed after her. Then, after a few awkward seconds, everyone left.

Except for me.

Alex seemed lost in thought, but after a few seconds, he seemed to realize I was still there.

"Hey," he said.

"Hey," I said back.

"So ... I just want to say it was really nice to meet you, Chloe."

"It was nice to meet you, too." My heart squeezed tight, making my breath catch. "I hope you have a good time at boarding school."

"Thanks."

Then there was a quiet moment as we looked at each other.

"I have something for you," he said. "Hold on. I'll go get it."

He went down the hall, and a few moments later he reappeared, holding a thick binder. He handed it to me, and I took it with both hands.

"It's my stories," he said. "I wanted you to have them."

I could only nod because I knew that if I tried to

speak, I would start crying. It wasn't lost on me that he'd decided to share what he considered something deeply personal with me.

It just made me love him more.

"Thank you," I said, my voice catching. "I'll take good care of this."

Our goodbye was simple. We didn't hug. I didn't cry. We just said goodbye to each other, and then I left.

When I got home, I went to my room, trying to hold my tears in. I sat on my bed and placed the binder in front of me.

Then, with a deep breath, I opened it.

There was a loose note there, before the first page.

It simply said, "This is me."

CHAPTER NINE

Alex's binder came to be my most prized possession. I read through it dozens of times over the past nine months. I had expected a collection of short stories, but it was more than that. There were also poems, drawings, and song lyrics of varying quality he apparently felt strongly enough about "a dozen chicks in tight shorts" to write lyrics about it .

I liked the stories the most because I got a sense of what was important to Alex. At first, I saw only adventure in them, what was on the surface, but the more I read them, the more I recognized certain themes. His stories were almost always about strong female characters faced with hard choices and tests of loyalty. They had to make sacrifices to keep the things that were important to them. My favorite was a story titled *Jenna's Choice*, which was about a teen girl living in a big fantasy city who takes on an evil cult to save her little brother and prevent the assassination of the Prince. In the process, she has to give up the stable life she's worked hard to build. Those types of stories showed me that Alex saw loyalty and friendship as things worth fighting for. Things worth making sacrifices for. I saw in those stories his conviction and strength.

The poems had been a surprise. Some of them were humorously bad—like one about a wizard mosquito—but most were serious, and showed me that Alex fixated on losing the things that were important to him. I often wondered if Alex doubted himself or if he was scared that he wouldn't be strong enough to fight for what he believed in. I began to see that his fear was his weakness.

I loved reading Alex's stories and poems because each time I read them, I learned something new about Alex. They were a window into his soul. Alex knew that I would see him, *really* see him, by reading his work. That he trusted me with his true self, his most intimate thoughts, made me feel like I was very special to him.

I knew that Alex saw something in me that went beyond his relationships with other girls. He chose to share his binder of stories with me—not Stacy, not London—just me. That gave me the strength to eventually let go of the jealousy I'd felt over Alex's relationship with Stacy. She might have known him longer and been sexually intimate with him, but she didn't have what Alex had given to me.

Despite all of that, though, I never let myself believe that Alex loved me. I knew I was important to him, but so was London. And what Alex had shown me in his writings, he had probably shared with her over the course of their relationship. It may not have been romantic, but I knew Alex loved London, and that she knew him in a way I probably never would.

I didn't really know what it meant. I knew *what* Alex had done by sharing his stories with me, but I could never figure out *why* he had done it. I didn't know where I stood with him, or what I was to him, and that bothered me. I got so worked up about it that I swore to myself that when I saw Alex again, I would do my best to act as if he had never given me his binder. I didn't want to assume something about the way he felt about me only to be proven wrong. That would be humiliating and painful. I was dying to talk to him about his stories, to find out more about what they meant to him and why he had written them, but I didn't want to come across as a clingy, lovesick girl who had stupidly assumed that the boy she was in love with loved her back.

That was the main reason I had gotten together with Ryan, and why I had stayed with him for five months. I didn't want to put my life on hold and pine over Alex as if he had made a promise to me. So when

Ryan had asked me to be his girlfriend, I had said yes. He was sweet and cute, and I liked him. We shared a common interest that was important to both of us, so it seemed like it could work.

But it didn't. I was always thinking of Alex, reading his stories, and learning more about him. I wanted to be with him, not Ryan. Despite that, though, I stayed with Ryan and did my best to return his affection. I was even sexual with him. We never had sex, but I'd had firsts with him I never would have anticipated reaching when we first got together.

Eventually, though, I began to feel really bad about how I was using Ryan. I didn't love him. I wasn't even all that attracted to him. I was just with him because he was a means to an end. When it became clear that he—through no fault of his own—couldn't give me what I selfishly wanted, I broke up with him.

And I went back to obsessing about how things would be between Alex and me when he came back. Would he treat me the same way he had last summer? Would he still think of me? Want to get to know me? More importantly, would he acknowledge the bond between us that came from reading his stories? I liked to think that he would. I hoped that he would confide in me and share himself with me, putting me above all others.

Was that selfish and naïve? Probably, but I couldn't help wanting it.

Now, with my ninth-grade year over and summer

just beginning, I waited anxiously for Alex to come back home. To come back to me.

It was Wednesday night, the Saudi equivalent of Friday in the States, one week after school had ended, and we were hanging out at Anna's house because her parents were out for the night. The idea had been to have a small party to see Ryan and Matt off, who were leaving the following morning. They were the last of our friends to move back to the States for good. Only me, Anna, Avery, and Stacy would be left. Just us four.

In a way, I felt like I had lost a part of myself because I'd grown so close to the kids who I'd spent my ninth grade year with. There'd been so few of us living here that we spent all of our time together. We hadn't really had a choice; there was no one else to hang out with. We couldn't help but get close, and get to know each other really well. I even became good friends with Stacy, who was someone I probably never would have spent time with if we'd been back in the US.

It was like this one thing we all had in common— living here together in such a small, tight-knit community with only each other to spend time with— had forged bonds that went beyond friendship.

With this weighing on all our minds, you could hardly call our little gathering a party. No one seemed to be in a festive mood.

I'd been idly sipping at a cup of grape soda, leaning

against the dining room wall, when Ryan came up to me.

"Can I talk to you? Outside?"

Not this again

I pushed off the wall. "Sure."

"Let's go out back."

I followed him out the sliding glass patio doors, and we stood in the warm, dark night, facing each other.

"What is it, Ryan?"

"I ... I'm going to miss you."

"Me, too. It's been really nice knowing you."

He let out a bitter laugh. "Is that all? Just nice? Didn't it mean anything more to you?"

I sighed. "Ryan, we've been over this. I explained it all when I broke up with you. You said you understood."

"I know," he said. "It's just that ... I guess you meant more to me than I did to you."

I didn't answer.

"Can I kiss you?" he asked.

I put a hand out to stop him when I saw he was starting to lean forward. "No," I said holding him back. "No kissing."

He nodded, looking hurt.

"But," I said, then drew him in. "We can have a goodbye hug." I wrapped my arms around him, and he did the same to me. "I'm really sorry I hurt you, Ryan. I really am."

We pulled apart after holding each other tight. I could see that his eyes brimmed with unshed tears.

"It's okay," he said. "I understand."

We stood there awkwardly for a few moments before he spoke again. "I'm going to go. Say goodbye to the girls for me. I just ... I just need to go." He walked over to the patio door that led to gravel yard behind the house and opened it. Before he stepped through, he turned to face me. "I loved you."

"Goodbye, Ryan."

And he left.

I stood there for a few minutes, regretting that I had gotten together with Ryan in the first place. I should have waited for Alex. I should have remained true to my feelings for him. Maybe he didn't see me the way I saw him—maybe he never would—but I loved him, and I felt as if I had tarnished that love by being with Ryan. All the firsts I'd experienced with Ryan—especially the sexual ones—I wished had been with Alex instead.

Oh well

Sighing, I turned and went back inside.

The girls and Matt asked where Ryan had gone, so I told them and passed along his farewells. Not long after, we said goodbye to Matt, gave him hugs, and then he left, too.

We all made our way to the living room and sat on the sofa and chairs.

"So," Anna said.

"So," I replied.

"I guess it's just us now," she said, looking at each of us. "I feel sad."

"There's the boarding school kids," Stacy supplied. "They're coming back for the summer."

"Alex," Anna said, voicing my thoughts. "And Hudson and London. Maybe Logan, too. They said they'd be back."

"It's going to be so boring this summer," Stacy moaned.

"It has to be better than last summer," Anna said. "It was just me and Stacy and Avery. Talk about being bored. At least if Alex, Hudson, and London come back, we'll have more people to do stuff with."

"You mean hang out at the pool all day and then do nothing at night?" I asked.

"Well, no ... " She paused. "I just mean it'll be something new. They can tell us about boarding school and stuff. And maybe they can get us booze. I wish they'd left us some."

Not long after that, we all went back to our houses.

The next day we all gathered at the pool. We did our usual routine of laying out on the lounge chairs and going into the water every now and then when we got hot. Then when we got hungry, we had our snack bar food at one of the picnic tables.

We were in the middle of lunch when Anna suddenly stood up, looking toward the back entrance to the pool area. "It's Hudson!"

Anna and I jumped up and ran over to him. "Hudson!" Anna squealed and then gave him a hug. "You're back!"

"Hey, Anna. Chloe. Yeah, I'm back. It's good to see you guys again."

I could tell right away that there was something off. There was something hanging over him like he wasn't sure how to deal with us.

Of course, I had only one thought. "Where's Alex?" Hudson and Alex went to the same boarding school. Wouldn't they have come back on the same flight? Shouldn't Alex be here too?

Hudson's smile disappeared, and he looked down at the ground, his face turning pensive. "He's at his house. He didn't want to come out."

What?

I immediately went back to get my stuff.

"Where are you going?" Anna asked me.

"To see Alex."

At my chaise, I slipped into my shorts and put on my top, gathered up my stuff and walked back to Hudson and Anna.

"Chloe," Hudson said, reaching out to stop me. "Wait."

"What is it?"

"Listen," he said, pulling me to the side, so we had some privacy, then paused like he was choosing his words carefully. "He's changed."

"What do you mean?"

Hudson looked past my shoulder, his lips pursed as he thought. "Just don't be surprised, okay?"

I looked at him, not really sure what he was getting at, then I nodded and left.

It didn't take long to get to Alex's house because he lived right next to the division that separated the housing area from the commons, right by the movie theater.

I knocked on the door and waited.

Then the door opened, and Alex stood before me. Suddenly I knew what Hudson had meant.

Alex's eyes, his beautiful eyes, were dead. The life and energy that had always fascinated me were gone, leaving behind an emptiness and sadness that was shocking to see.

And he looked tired like he hadn't slept in days.

"Oh," he said, his lips flat and emotionless. "Hi, Chloe."

That was it? Just a 'Hi, Chloe'? We hadn't seen each other in nine months, and now all he could muster was a lackluster greeting?

"Hi, Alex. Can I come in?"

He stepped back, opening the door wide for me. "Yeah, come in."

I followed him into his house, and we sat on the sofa together, with a full cushion between us.

"Are you okay?" I asked.

A short, bitter laugh escaped him. "I guess you could say I've been better."

I certainly believed that. He didn't look all that well with his loose shorts, wrinkled T-shirt, and messy hair. It was like he couldn't be bothered to look after himself. Like he didn't care.

"Did something happen?" I asked carefully.

He remained silent for a moment, then spoke. "So how was your ninth-grade year?" he asked, totally ignoring my question.

That was a big question to ask. How was my year living on this tiny compound in the middle of nowhere with only a few kids as your friends? Life changing? "Well, I guess I know now what it's like to grow up here. I understand some of the things you told me last summer."

"Yeah. I figured you would."

"Will you come out with me? The girls would like to see you."

"The girls? Who's left?"

"Me, Anna and Stacy and Avery."

"That's it?"

"Yeah," I said. "Everyone else left."

"Wow. I guess it's going to be wild and crazy this summer."

"So will you come to the pool with me?"

He ran his hand through his hair, making it messier, and then he sighed. "Nah. I don't think so. I'm pretty tired. I didn't sleep all that well. I'll come out later tonight." He stood, walked to the door and held it open. "You should go," he said, his tone making it clear that he wanted me to leave.

He was kicking me out? What the hell?

I stood and made my way to the door, barely able to hide my disappointment. "Okay. I'll see you later, I guess. I'm glad you're back. I missed you."

He nodded, his eyes gazing past my shoulder. "Yeah. Me too. I missed you, too." And, finally, there was emotion in his voice, something there to let me know that, maybe, he'd thought of me.

I stepped out, closed the door, and all but ran back to the pool.

I found Hudson and the girls at the picnic table talking. I stood by Hudson until he looked up at me. There was a simple understanding in his eyes, an acknowledgment that something sad had just happened.

"I need to talk to you," I said. "Alone."

Anna looked at me, concern etched into her features, her eyes asking me what had happened. I glanced back at her, trying to let her know that we'd talk later.

Hudson nodded. "Yeah. Okay. Over here."

He walked me to the far end of the pavilion by the kiddie pool, and we sat together at a table, facing each other.

"I told you," he said sadly.

"What happened?" I demanded. "What happened to him? Why is he like that?"

Hudson remained quiet for a long time, looking

past my shoulder. I waited. Then he took in a big breath and exhaled slowly. "Alex had a girlfriend back at school," he said, and a painful flutter brushed past my heart, a tinge of jealousy, which was ridiculous. Alex and I hadn't been a couple. I didn't have a claim on him. And it wasn't like I hadn't been with someone, too. There was no reason for me to expect that Alex wouldn't have had a girlfriend. "This girl Taylor. They were together for a while."

"Did they break up?" I asked. "Is he sad because she left him?"

"No," Hudson said, looking down at his hands that were clasped in front of him. "She didn't break up with him. She ... "

I sat there, anxiously, waiting for him to continue, but he didn't.

"She what?"

Finally, Hudson looked at me, and there was sorrow in his eyes. "She died. And he was with her when it happened."

Oh my god

I suddenly felt ashamed for being so irritated with Alex. "That's horrible."

Hudson's eyes shifted over my shoulder again. "It happened about two months ago."

"Do you ... do you know what happened to her?"

He nodded and kept quiet for a few moments. "They went out on the mountain together one weekend. Hiking. They were climbing a cliff, and she fell off."

I felt my eyes begin to water. I couldn't even imagine what that must have been like for him, what he must have gone through. What he was still obviously going through.

"Don't let him know I told you," Hudson said. "And don't tell anyone else. I only told you because ... actually, I'm not sure why I told you. I just felt you needed to know. Just keep this between us, okay? He wouldn't want anyone to know. Back at school, *everyone* knew, and he hated it."

"Okay," I said, my voice rough. "Thanks for telling me. I won't tell anyone. I promise."

"Good," he said, then smiled at me. "It's good to see you again, by the way. And despite what you might have seen today, Alex is glad to see you again too."

"Really?" I wasn't sure I believed that, given how Alex had just been acting toward me.

"Yeah. He mentioned you pretty often. Even after he got together with Taylor. He thought about you a lot."

Had he really? Wouldn't he have been at least a little bit excited to see me then? Or was he just too caught up in the tragedy of what had happened to his girlfriend to be able to reach out to me that way? That was something I could understand, but it didn't take the sting over Alex's cold reception away.

CHAPTER TEN

Later that night, Anna came over to my house, and we walked together toward the commons, ready for another boring night of hanging out and not doing much of anything. Like usual.

"Are you going to tell me what happened today?" she asked as we walked.

I stopped walking, and when she did as well, I grabbed her by the shoulders. She looked at me, surprised. "I love you, Anna. You're the best friend I've ever had. But I can't tell you. I promised I wouldn't. I'm sorry."

"Hey, girl," she said, smiling. "It's okay. I get it. If you made a promise, I don't want you to break it. I just wanted to know if you're okay."

We resumed our walk.

"Are you?" she asked. "You've been kind of freaked all day long."

"I'm not sure," I told her.

We found Stacy and Avery on the swings at the playground, and they waved us over as we approached. We waved back.

It had taken a couple of months for me to be comfortable around Stacy, but eventually, we became good friends. I began to understand her, at least enough for me to get over the differences that had at first kept us from bonding. Stacy didn't have much self-confidence, and she compensated by projecting a rough exterior. Once I understood that, I began to open up to her, trying to let her know that she didn't have to be that way with me. And she got it. She understood. And I knew she appreciated it.

And then there was Avery. It had taken longer to get close to her because she was a quiet girl. Not really shy, just private. She usually only spoke when she was required to. And the way she just simply *observed* everything around her was sort of intimidating. That had taken some getting used to.

She and Stacy were best friends, and they were always together. Avery seemed to get Stacy, understand her on some level that the rest of us didn't. She was always looking after her, comforting Stacy when she was hating herself. Avery was really in sync with Stacy's moods. She seemed to always know when to be there for her and when to back off.

They were like twins.

"Hey," Stacy called us over. "Have you guys seen Alex?"

Of course, that's the first thing she'd want to know. She was still obsessed with him and had probably been waiting for him to come back as eagerly as I had.

"No, just Hudson," Anna said. "Let's go to the bleachers. I want to get some fries at the snack bar."

About an hour later, after it had gotten dark and the softball field lights had been turned on, we were sitting on the bleachers when we saw Alex and Hudson walking over toward us.

They were each holding a large bottle of Mirinda, and I knew with certainty that there was sadiki in them, which surprised me because after they'd left last summer, the alcohol had disappeared. There hadn't been a hint of alcohol throughout my ninth-grade year. How was it that they'd got hold of sadiki when they hadn't even been here for a day?

"Hey, girls," Hudson said as they came over. "Keeping busy, I see." He laughed at his own joke.

I studied Alex. He'd put himself together, and he looked marginally better. His eyes, though, were still lifeless.

"Hi, Alex," Stacy cooed, giving him obvious flirty eyes.

"Hey," he said back, but he didn't even look at her.

Stacy's brow furrowed, but she didn't say anything.

We watched them as they settled down next to us.

"Is that sadiki?" Stacy asked.

"Yep," Hudson answered.

"Where did you get it?" I asked, still curious.

"316," he said. "It's still empty, and our stash is still there. There's tons of it."

That surprised me. In a bolder moment this past spring, some of us had sneaked into 316 just to check it out, but we hadn't seen a stash of alcohol there. It was kind of weird being there because it sort of felt like someone still lived there; even the beds were made.

"Share?" Stacy asked Alex, holding out her hand. He shrugged, then handed his bottle over. She took a few swigs then nearly choked, grimacing. "Crap, that's strong."

Anna reached for the bottle next, giving me an apologetic look like she didn't want me to be disappointed that she was going to drink. She, too, made a scrunched-up face when she took a drink.

When the bottle was passed back to Alex, he took it and had several big gulps. I looked to Hudson, but he just shrugged back at me.

"So what are we going to do?" I asked.

Alex snorted. "I don't know what you guys are going to do, but I know what I'm going to do."

"And what is that?" Stacy asked, still trying to be flirty.

"Get very, very drunk," he said, then took more big swallows.

He was already well on his way.

I looked back to Hudson, giving him a concerned

look, but he just shrugged again, as if to say, "This is nothing new, and I don't know what to do about it."

Anna touched my shoulder, and when she caught my eye, I could see that there was an understanding there. She was beginning to piece things together. But like Hudson, I was only able to provide a shrug.

We sat uncomfortably after that, not knowing what to say in the face of Alex's black mood.

Finally, Stacy stood. "Bathroom," she said, and she and Avery headed off to the girls' locker room.

When they came back, Stacy climbed the bleachers and sat next to Alex, then she leaned over and whispered something to him.

Avery sat where she'd been sitting before and stared off into the distance, her expression unreadable.

Alex and Stacy sat huddled together and shared the bottle of sadiki between them. Anna made her way over to sit by Hudson and me, and she had more to drink. When Hudson offered me the bottle, I just shook my head, and he let it pass.

I looked back at Alex. "Don't you think you've had enough?"

"Not nearly," he replied, somewhat abruptly, and I couldn't help but feel a little bit hurt. Especially since he didn't seem to mind being so close to Stacy.

I did my best to hide it, but jealousy burned through me. I should have seen this coming. I should have known that he'd pick up with Stacy right where they'd left off. Was making out with her all he wanted to do?

Stacy whispered something else to him, and he listened intently. Then he nodded. The two of them stood, and Stacy had to steady Alex as they made their way down the bleachers because he was swaying so much.

"Where are you guys going?" I asked when they got to the ground.

"Wherever," Alex replied, then stumbled away with Stacy's arm around his waist.

So they were going off to be alone. Just like last summer.

At least this time I was pretty sure they weren't going to have sex. Stacy had told me in a rare moment of openness that she was a virgin and that the furthest she'd ever gone was third base. She'd done it with more than one boy, including Alex.

I couldn't judge her, though, because I'd done the same with Ryan.

After they'd left, Anna looked at us, perplexed. "What the hell?"

We all looked to Hudson, but he only tightened his lips and shook his head slightly. "Yeah ... "

The next day, late in the morning, Anna and I went to see Alex at his house.

"You don't need to tell me," she said as we walked. "I'm figuring it out."

I didn't have to ask what she was talking about. "I knew you would."

When we got to Alex's house, I knocked on the door.

There was no answer, so I knocked again, louder.

"Do you think he already went out?" Anna asked.

"After he drank so much last night? I don't think so."

"Well, if he's in, he'll be alone. His dad is at work. And I know his mom is in the States with his older sister. Try the door."

I pushed down on the handle to find it unlocked. "Should we go in?"

"Yes."

I opened the door, and we both stepped in.

"Alex?" I called out quietly.

No answer.

Anna and I looked at each other. "His room?"

I nodded, then both of us walked down the hallway that led to the bedrooms. All of the family homes on the compound were exactly alike, right down to the furniture, so I knew which bedroom would be his.

The door was closed.

I knocked and called out his name again. "Alex?"

There was no response.

"Open the door." Anna urged.

I pushed down on the handle, and the door swung quietly open. We stepped in to find Alex asleep on his stomach, tangled in his sheets. He was shirtless.

"Alex?" I said. He barely stirred, so I tried again, louder this time. "Alex."

His head snapped up, and he looked around, his eyes squinted and bleary. He groaned and dropped his head back down on his pillow. "What are you guys doing here?"

"We came to get your hungover ass out of bed," Anna said, then moved to the window and threw open the drapes, letting the sunlight stream in.

Alex groaned again. "This is cruel and unusual punishment," he said, and I was surprised to hear a note of humor in his voice.

"Come on," she urged. "Get up. We're going to the pool."

"Ugh," he said, then in one fluid motion he sat up, then stood, rubbing his eyes.

Anna and I both gasped, our eyes wide.

Alex was completely naked. And he had an erection. And ... wow, it was big.

"I'm taking a shower," he said, seemingly unaware of his nudity. "I'll be right out."

Then he walked out of his room, into the bathroom, and shut the door.

Anna and I turned to each other, our eyes still wide.

"Did you see that?" Anna asked.

I nodded, not knowing what else to say.

"I didn't know they got that big," she said, sounding amazed. "Did you?"

While she had never seen a penis, for some reason she suspected I had I had , so she was looking for some sort of confirmation. "No," I said. "I didn't."

"Oh my god, I can't believe that just happened."

Soon, we heard the shower turn off, and after a few minutes, Alex emerged and came into the room, a towel tied around his waist.

"I'll just get changed," he said.

"We'll wait out front," I yelped when it became clear that he was going to get naked in front of us again. I grabbed Anna by the arm and dragged her out of the room, closing the door behind us.

In the living room, Anna giggled. "He was going to do it again!"

"It's not funny, Anna. That's not normal behavior. He shouldn't be doing that. That was like sexual assault."

"I'm sorry," she said, looking sheepish. "You're right. It's just that I've never seen one."

"Well, now you have."

Alex came out a few minutes later, dressed in swim trunks and a black tank top. He looked much better than he had the night before. He looked ... almost normal. That desperate look, what I had come to realize was pain, was gone. He even wore a half-smile, though it didn't reach his eyes. They were still flat.

I stood in front of him, waiting for an apology. He

just looked back at me, confused. "What?"

"That was really rude," I said, letting him know I wasn't pleased. "What makes you think I want to see your dick? You shouldn't have done that."

An odd expression came over him like he was puzzling things out, like he was going over the last hour in his head, trying to recall what he'd done. "Oh. Shit. I, uh, okay, I'm sorry. You're right. I shouldn't have done that. But I didn't quite realize I was naked when I got out of bed. I was kind of dazed. I'm sorry."

"I didn't mind," Anna squeaked out behind me.

I snapped my head back to her and glared until she looked down at the floor. "Sorry," she said, but I could tell she wasn't.

I turned my attention back to Alex. "Don't do it again."

"I'm sorry," he said again. "I won't."

"Okay. Are you ready?"

"Um, I have to do some chores first," he said, moving to the kitchen.

We followed behind him. He stopped by the stove and picked up a piece of paper. "See?" he said, holding it out to me.

There was a list of tasks on it like doing the dishes, picking up the house, cleaning up his room, things like that.

"We'll do the stuff out here," I said, taking the list from him. "You go take care of your room."

"You sure?"

"Do you want to do it all yourself?"

"Okay, okay. Thanks."

I don't know what took him so long—his room hadn't seemed that messy to me—but Anna and I finished our tasks several minutes before he came back.

"Let's go," I said, and we left his house.

My annoyance had pretty much dissipated by the time we arrived at the pool. In fact, Alex's mood was so much better than the previous night that I found myself smiling.

Stacy, Avery, and Hudson were already at the pool eating lunch. After getting our own food, we sat with them at their picnic table.

"Hey guys," I said.

I glanced at Hudson, and he nodded and smiled at me, as if to say, "He's doing okay today."

Afterward, we laid out our towels at the area Stacy and Avery had already claimed, and we soaked up the sun.

"So what's boarding school like?" Anna asked the boys.

Immediately, the smile faded from Alex's face, and he looked down.

I caught Anna's eye and shook my head at her, trying to make it clear that she shouldn't have asked that.

But Hudson took control and began to tell us about his experience at boarding school. He told us all about what it was like to live there, boarding with so many other students, living with his teachers. We asked a lot of questions, and he did his best to answer us. It all seemed so exotic, so different from anything I knew. They'd done so much, experienced so many things.

As Hudson talked, I began to understand why he seemed different than from the previous summer. Boarding school had changed him, matured him. He'd grown beyond the limitations of what he'd known before. I wondered if that had happened to Alex, too.

"Did you guys have girlfriends?" Stacy asked at one point, and a panicked feeling ran through me. Hudson visibly flinched.

"I'm getting in the pool," Alex said, breaking his silence, and he left us.

Stacy noticed Hudson's reaction. "What? Did I say something wrong?"

Hudson looked at her, trying to put her at ease. "No, it's okay. Alex had a girlfriend, but he had a bad experience with her. He doesn't like to talk about it."

"Oh," Stacy said, then stood. She walked to the edge of the pool, jumped in, then swam over to where Alex was paddling water in the deep end.

I was impressed how Hudson had handled that, and how he'd managed not to lie.

When Alex and Stacy came back about a half hour later, he seemed to be okay again, but there was no emotion on his face. I was more than a bit surprised when he came over to sit by me.

Stacy watched it all, a hurt expression on her face.

CHAPTER ELEVEN

The next morning, I went to Alex's house again, but by myself.

When I got there, I knocked on the door, not really expecting Alex to answer it. It was unlocked, so I entered the house. When I didn't see Alex, I made my way back to his room, pushing the door open and stepping in.

He was asleep, this time on his back. He was shirtless again.

"Alex?"

I wondered if he was hungover again. He hadn't had much to drink the night before, at least not while I'd been around, but I had to go home at eleven. I knew he could stay out later. He might have gone somewhere with Hudson or Stacy to drink more.

"Alex!"

He sat up, but thankfully, didn't stand up. "I didn't mean to," he said, looking confused like he didn't know where he was or how he got there. Then he noticed me. "Oh. Hi, Chloe."

"Hey, Alex."

He swiveled his legs over the side of the bed and threw the sheets to the side.

I spun around, and I heard a snort behind me.

"Relax. I'm not naked."

I still didn't turn around. "I'll wait for you up front."

In the kitchen, another list of chores lay on the counter. I heard Alex start the shower, so I figured I would pass the time taking care of his to-dos. It was all pretty easy stuff, and by the time Alex came out of the bathroom, I had finished off the list.

When he joined me in the kitchen and looked around. "You cleaned up," he said. "Why did you do that?"

"I was bored," I said.

"Oh. Well, thanks. I hate doing chores. You're the best." He gave me a half-smile like he just didn't have it in him to smile fully.

I was glad to see that he seemed to be in a fairly good mood. I could tell that he was still off, that he wasn't quite normal, but he wasn't nearly as bad off as he'd been that first night.

We spent the day at the pool like we usually did and would certainly do the rest of the summer. We laid out in the sun, we played in the pool, and we had lunch under the pavilion. Alex stayed close to me throughout the day, and I could tell that that bothered Stacy by the hurt I saw on her face, but she didn't seem to be angry with me about it. Maybe she saw that it wasn't anything I had any control over. I couldn't tell Alex what to do, and I certainly wasn't going to push him away.

I didn't feel bad about it, though. In fact, I rather liked it. It reminded me of how Alex had paid attention to me last summer.

But I wasn't sure what it meant. I didn't know what he was trying to tell me, if anything, by the way he was treating me. I wasn't even sure if he was aware of it himself.

That night, after we'd gone home, checked in with the parents and had dinner, the girls gathered at the bleachers.

We had no idea where Alex and Hudson were, so we just sat around talking.

An hour later, the boys showed up, each of them with their bottles. By the sway in their walk, I could tell they'd already been drinking.

I studied Alex as he approached. He still seemed ... okay. Not bad, but not great either. His face wasn't quite expressionless, but he wasn't smiling.

Stacy moved to join him, and without a word, he handed his bottle over to her.

I watched, annoyed, as she leaned in and whispered in his ear. He actually cracked a smile. He said something back to her, but I couldn't hear it.

Alex didn't drink so much that night. The bottle stayed at his side, but he only drank from it occasionally. I could tell he was buzzed, but not drunk. For the most part, he sat quietly next to Stacy, whispering to her and sharing his bottle with her.

Suddenly, Alex got up and climbed up on the thin railing at the top of the bleachers.

"What are you doing?" Hudson asked, alarmed. "Get down, Alex. You're going to hurt yourself."

He didn't reply. Instead, he worked to balance himself on the railing, his arms wide and flailing. No one moved. I think we were too afraid we might distract him, knowing that he could really hurt himself if he fell. The drop to the hard gravel below was at least twelve feet.

"Get down," Stacy pleaded, her eyes wide with fear. "You're going to fall."

"I'm only going to fall if you get in the way." He turned and almost lost his balance. We all stood in alarm, watching as his limbs flailed wildly until he regained his balance.

"Get down, jackass," Hudson said. "I mean it."

"Quiet." Alex hissed. "You guys are going to make me fuck this up." He slowly began to make his way along the railing.

"Alex, please get down," I said, finally finding my voice.

Then he turned to face us, his back to the drop, and he tilted his head back.

I screamed first.

Alex fell back, then launched himself into the air. He sailed straight out as he tucked in his legs and his body twisted into a flip.

I stood there, stunned, my heart in my throat, as Alex hit the ground hard, barely making the back flip. His landing was off, and he fell backward on his arm. We rushed down the bleachers and back to where Alex lay, expecting to find that he'd broken his arm.

But when we reached him, he was splayed out on his back, laughing quietly. His left arm was torn up and scratched, and he was bleeding from several scrapes.

I was furious.

And so was everyone else.

"What the fuck!" Hudson shouted at Alex. "Are you fucking crazy? You could have killed yourself!"

Alex rose, his facing going hard. "Well, I didn't." He casually inspected his bleeding arm.

"You're an asshole!" Stacy screamed at him, then turned and ran away. Avery followed after.

Alex turned his attention from his arm to the rest of us, who stood staring at him. "What?" he asked like he hadn't just scared the crap out of all of us.

"Jesus," Hudson said, running a hand over his face in frustration. "What is wrong with you? You need to get over it, Alex. You can't keep doing shit like this."

Alex looked off into the night sky for several seconds. I watched as tears began to streak down his face. Finally, his eyes settled on Hudson. "Fuck you," he whispered, then he turned and left us.

I watched him go.

The next morning, I went to Alex's house to wake him up.

The front door, like usual, was unlocked, so I walked in. Not finding Alex in the living area, I walked to the hall.

I stopped half-way to Alex's room when I heard ... I wasn't sure what I heard, but it scared me. I burst into his room.

"Alex?" When I saw him, I gasped, and pain clenched my heart.

Alex was curled up on the floor in the far corner of his room, dressed only in his boxers. He held his knees and arms close to him as he rocked back and forth.

Horrible, wracking sobs shook his whole body. He cried like there was a terrible pain inside him, and it was clawing its way out of his body, ripping and tearing as it tore out of him.

For a brief moment, I stood watching him, too stunned to move. I'd never seen anything like that in my life. I didn't know a person could make the tortured sounds that were coming from Alex. I didn't know anyone could hurt as much as he appeared to be hurting.

"Oh my god," I said as the rational part of my

brain finally kicked into action. I rushed to him, knelt down, and pulled him close. He threw himself into me, almost knocking me down, and the most horrible wail tore out of him. I held him as tightly as I could because it was all I could do. He was shaking so much, I could barely hold on.

It took me a few moments to realize that Alex was trying to get words out between the sobs. "It was an accident," he managed to say amid all his sobbing. "I didn't mean to do it. It was an accident."

I had no idea what he was talking about, and I couldn't spare the energy to figure it out. I tried to lean back against the wall but fell back awkwardly, my butt landing hard on the floor. I pulled Alex down, so his head rested on my lap, and he drew his knees to his chest in a fetal position.

"It's okay," I whispered, knowing that it really wasn't. "It's okay. I'm here." I stroked his head, running my palm over his hair. "I'm here."

Alex's answer was a keening, gut-wrenching wail that crushed my heart. His pain was so great that it invaded my body, making my throat tighten. I wasn't surprised to feel tears track down my own cheeks.

Eventually, Alex's sobbing ebbed to an occasional pain-filled moan and hiccups that shook his body. Every now and then he would whisper, "It was an accident ... I didn't mean to do it."

I didn't know what he was talking about, so I continued to stroke his hair, whispering soothing words to him, reminding him that I was there with him, that he wasn't alone.

Finally, after about an hour, the sobs and moans subsided, and Alex's breathing became deep and rhythmic.

Then he sat up, faced away from me, and rubbed at his eyes.

"I need to take a shower," he said, then stood and walked out of the room, leaving me feeling like my own heart had been ripped open.

I heard the shower start, and not knowing what else to do, I made Alex's bed then went to the kitchen to start working on his chores.

I'd just finished when Alex appeared, dressed in shorts and a baggy, wrinkled T-shirt. His eyes, still puffy and red, were downcast, and he had a sad, defeated look on his face.

"Where's your first-aid kit?" I asked him.

He didn't say anything.

"Alex," I said, pushing at his shoulder. "Where is your first-aid kit?"

"Under the sink."

After pulling it out, I took out some gauze and soaked it with antiseptic solution. "This might hurt a little."

He didn't answer.

"Give me your arm."

As I was cleaning his scrapes, I studied him, my heart aching. But I was angry, too, about the stunt he had pulled the previous night.

"You're an idiot," I said to him, rubbing at his scrapes harder than was necessary. "What you did last night was really stupid."

"It turned out okay," he mumbled.

"It could have turned out very badly. You could have broken something. Or worse. You scared the crap out of us."

"Sorry."

"Please don't do anything like that again," I said shortly, trying to make my anger clear.

"I don't want to go out," he said, ignoring me. "Will you stay here with me?"

"Do you have food?"

"Yeah. Stuff to make sandwiches, I think."

"Okay."

I finished patching him up, then led him to the living room and sat him down on the sofa. "I'll make some sandwiches, okay?"

"Okay. Thanks."

Not only was there stuff to make sandwiches in the fridge, but there was also a big, covered bowl of potato salad. I wondered if Alex or his dad had made it. It only took a few minutes to make the sandwiches. Alex was sitting on the sofa with his elbows on his knees, his head in his hands. "Here you go." I placed his plate on the coffee table in front of him.

"Thanks."

I brought my food out, and slid in next to Alex on

the sofa.

As we ate in silence, I wondered about what I had witnessed. I didn't really know what to make of it. Clearly, Alex was hurting terribly about something, and I guessed it was about the death of his girlfriend. He probably loved her. Was still in love with her. And her death had scarred him.

Even though I could understand that, I had this persistent feeling that it went beyond that. I'd seen and heard more than grief. There had been something dark and frightening there.

And what had he meant about it being an accident? That he hadn't meant to do ... whatever it was he thought he did? Did he somehow feel guilty for not being able to save her? Hudson said that Alex and Taylor had been on the mountain, hiking. Did that mean that they were alone and far away from his town? If so, there wouldn't have been anyone around to help them. They would have been alone. There was nothing he could have done.

I shook my head. I was just speculating, trying to satisfy my own need to understand Alex's pain because now it had become my pain. My heart hurt for him. After holding him as he cried, my soul had been touched by his agony, and I knew I would never be able to forget it.

CHAPTER TWELVE

When we finished lunch, I took the dishes to the kitchen and cleaned up. Alex was still sitting, leaning back against the sofa cushion, and staring blankly ahead of him.

I sat next to him, close enough that our thighs touched.

"Alex," I said softly and put my hand on his leg, trying to reassure him. "Do you want to tell me what that was all about?"

I was surprised when he grabbed my hand and laced his fingers with mine. "Will you stay with me?"

Okay. He was ignoring my question. He didn't want to talk about it.

"Yes. I'll stay with you. Is there anything you'd like to do? Maybe play a game? Watch TV?"

"Can you ... "

I leaned forward, tilted my head up so I could look at him. "What is it? Tell me. I want to help."

"I want you to hold me again. Please."

"Okay." Alex was quite a bit taller than me, and I was too short to hold him the way we were sitting, so I scooted over and pulled him toward me, so his head rested on my lap. He reached up with his hand, and I realized that he wanted me to hold it. I didn't hesitate. I played with his hair with my free hand, wanting him to know that I was with him.

We'd been sitting together like that, quietly, for almost an hour, when there was a knock on the door. Alex sat up but didn't move to answer it. Wanting to protect him, I answered it myself.

Anna was there with her goofy grin on.

"Hey, girl!" she said cheerfully. "I thought you might—" She saw the look on my face, and her eyes widened. "What happened? Is Alex okay?"

I wasn't going to tell Anna what had happened. In fact, I knew I wasn't going to tell anyone, ever. This was between Alex and me, and no one else.

I stepped out and closed the door behind me. "Anna ... I can't tell you. I promised."

She studied me for a few heartbeats. "Okay. I understand. Are you guys coming to the pool?"

"I don't think so. Alex isn't feeling well. Maybe we'll be out tonight."

She nodded, giving me a comforting smile. "Okay. I'll see you guys later then. Bye."

"Bye."

Inside, I found Alex where I'd left him, his head

hanging low, staring at nothing.

I walked over to him and grabbed his hand, and pulled. "Get up," I told him. "We're going to play a game or something. Where are your board games?"

"In my closet."

"Come on." I pulled him over to the dining room table and sat him down, then went to find a game.

Alex's mood improved slightly as we played Dungeon. He was more alert, but that terrible sadness was still in his eyes.

"I read your stories," I told him after we'd finished a game, wondering if he even remembered giving them to me.

"Did you like them?"

"I loved them, Alex. They're really good. *You're* really good. I've read them all dozens of times. It was really sweet of you to share them with me. Thank you."

"I wanted you to have them," he said, staring off at nothing. "I wanted you to know me."

I thought I did, even though we'd only been together for two weeks. But now ... now I felt like there was a vast gulf between us. I felt his pain, but I didn't understand it. And I felt like I really couldn't help him unless I did.

"Alex," I began carefully. I had to handle this gently. "Why were you crying?"

He sat in silence for nearly a minute, and I began to wonder if he would just ignore me.

"I had a girlfriend," he finally said, his gaze fixed straight ahead of him. "At boarding school. Her name was Taylor." He referred to her in the past tense. "She was a junior. I met her in my French class. We sat next to each and were paired off for a project once. After that, we hung out together. One day, kind of out of the blue, she asked me to be her boyfriend. I was surprised, you know? I mean, she was beautiful and older than me. I thought she could have any guy she wanted, but she chose me. So I said yes. We were together for most of the year. I ... I liked her. She made me laugh. She made me feel good. And she was my first."

I felt a stab of jealousy I didn't particularly know what to do with, but I kept quiet.

He took a deep breath and let it out in a big rush. His bottom lip began to tremble, and he struggled to stay in control of his emotions. When he regained his composure, he went on.

"About two months ago, we decided to go hiking on the mountain—because the snow was melting, you know? We were kind of tired of skiing and just wanted to do something different. So we went exploring on the mountain. We'd been out most of the day when we came up to this cliff. I wanted to climb it. She didn't. But I convinced her to. It was kind of scary. And we almost made it. I was almost at the top when Taylor started to get really scared. She said she was stuck. I ... I looked down at her. And that's when she fell. She fell all the way to the rocks on the bottom. And she just lay there."

The tears slipped free then, and he became quiet.

"I don't even know how I got to her or how long it took. But I found her there on the rocks. Her legs ... they ... her body was broken. There was so much blood, Chloe. It was all over her ... all over her face. But she was alive. She was breathing. And I just sat there next to her. I didn't know what to do. I didn't want to leave her. I knew she was dying, and I didn't want her to die alone, so I stayed with her. I stayed with her instead of getting help. I just didn't want her to be alone, you know?

"I held her until she died. I stayed there even after it got dark, even after it got really cold. I just held her. I kind of felt like she would wake up at any moment and she would need me. So I just ... stayed there with her.

"But eventually I realized that she wasn't coming back, that she was really dead. So I left her and went back down the mountain. I knocked at the first house I came to, and told the people there what happened."

When he didn't say any more, I reached out and took his hands.

"That's horrible, Alex," I said, trying to sound strong. "I'm so sorry you had to experience that. And I'm sorry that you lost someone close to you. But there was nothing you could have done. It wasn't your fault. You need to understand that."

Amazingly, he laughed, but it was ugly, bitter.

"I understand," he said, sitting up straighter and

rubbing his eyes. "I completely understand."

I instinctively knew that he was talking about something else, something he hadn't told me.

"Alex, I think you should—"

"Can we not talk about this anymore? I think I just want to be alone now."

I wasn't so sure that was a good idea, but I decided to respect his wishes. "Okay."

I left him then and went back to my house.

After dinner, the girls came over to get me. We ended up at the bleachers like usual, just talking because there wasn't anything else to do. We'd made our way to the playground and were hanging out on the jungle gym when we spotted the boys walking toward us.

They each had their bottles of Mirinda.

I was surprised to see that Alex seemed to be in a much better mood. He wasn't smiling, and his eyes were dull, but he was alert.

"Girls," Hudson said when they reached us. "What's shaking?"

"Oh, you know," Anna said in her cheerful voice. "The usual. Plotting world domination and such."

That made Stacy laugh.

"What about you guys?" Anna asked.

"Oh, you know," Alex said, mimicking Anna. "The usual. Enjoying a fine blend of sadiki and Mirinda." Then he did just that, taking a big swig from the bottle.

Stacy reached out, and he passed the bottle to her.

Hudson held his out to Anna, nodding for her to take it.

"Sure," she said, taking the bottle from him then drinking more than I would have expected.

I gave her a look.

She shrugged back at me. "Don't judge me. I'm *so* bored."

Alex headed off to the monkey bars, and we watched him. He stood underneath the bars, his back toward us. Then he slipped his T-shirt over his head and hung it up on one of the bars. He jumped up, grabbed a bar, then pulled himself up.

I watched, transfixed.

I'd seen Alex without a shirt plenty of times. And while he had an amazing body, and I'd sneaked glances here and there, I'd never seen his body displayed this way. As Alex pulled himself up, then lowered again, the muscles of his back and arms rippled under his skin. As a warmth grew low in my belly, I realized I'd never seen anything so sexy in my life. My hormones raged, and I found myself desperately wanting to be alone with him, touching him, kissing him. Doing more. A lot more.

"Wow," Anna breathed. "He's so ... "

"Hot," Stacy supplied.

"Yeah."

Hudson laughed from where he sat. "You guys are drooling."

Eventually, Alex stopped tormenting us girls and walked back to us, still shirtless, and breathing hard.

"Feel better?" Hudson asked him.

Alex nodded, then took his bottle back from Stacy. He uncapped it and took a long drink like he was drinking water.

"Tell us more about boarding school," Anna said.

It was obvious that Alex wasn't going to say anything, so Hudson began to tell us about a canoe trip in France that he'd been on. Then he told us about a class trip to Zurich that, somehow, involved prostitutes.

As Hudson was telling us about another class trip to Paris, Stacy jumped down from the jungle gym and went to sit next to Alex. She whispered in his ear, and I knew she was suggesting that they go off somewhere to make out or whatever. Alex pulled away from her slightly then looked over at me. She tried again, and once again Alex turned his attention to me like he was trying to decide something.

I simply looked back at him.

When Stacy put her arms around him and whispered into his ear again, he nodded. Then the two of them stood.

"Maybe we'll see you guys later," he said over his shoulder as he and Stacy walked away.

I was so jealous I wanted to scream.

What did he see in her? And why didn't he see that in me?

But I knew what it was. Stacy was willing to have casual sexual encounters with him. They'd been doing it for years. They'd even been boyfriend and girlfriend a few times. They had a history. She was something familiar to him.

And it wasn't like he had that kind of interest in me anyway. Even if he did, I wasn't going to be sexual with him unless we were together, and I didn't see that happening. Why would he be with me when he had a sure thing with Stacy? There were no strings attached with her.

And I could understand, I suppose, that something casual was the only thing Alex could commit to right now. It was all he had in him to give.

Whatever.

It didn't matter anyway. As much as I wanted him, as much as I wished it was me he was walking away with, I didn't want to just be a fling to him. I wanted him to love me the way I loved him.

But I didn't think he ever would.

CHAPTER THIRTEEN

Two days later, after having spent the morning at the pool and having lunch, we gathered at Alex's house to play board games. We were well into a game of Monopoly when there was a knock at the door.

Alex, who had been in a flat, lifeless mood, stood and walked over to the door. When he opened it, London rushed in and threw her arms around him, holding him tight and burying her face in his neck.

So quietly I almost didn't hear it, she whispered, "I'm so sorry. I'm so sorry."

Alex's arms moved slowly, hesitantly at first, but then he grabbed her and held her close.

They stood holding each other for long moments as we watched, not wanting to interrupt their reunion, and London continued to tell Alex how sorry she was.

Sorry for what? Did she know about Alex's girlfriend?

Hudson stood up then and made his way to Alex

and London. When she noticed him, she pulled away from Alex, her face wet, and gave him a hug, but it was quicker, less emotional than the hug she'd shared with Alex.

"I missed you guys so much," she said when she finally stepped back from them.

"Us, too," Hudson said as Alex pulled away, his head hanging low. "We missed you too. You look really great."

She did. In fact, she looked even more mature than she had last summer. There was something about the way she carried herself that spoke of a newfound confidence. She'd grown up over the past year, just like Hudson and Alex had.

And she still oozed sex. She was gorgeous in her tight shorts and top that hugged her body and showed off her womanly curves.

I found myself feeling self-conscious and jealous again.

When the three of them came back to the table, we all greeted London. She smiled at us, even at Stacy, but then she focused on Avery. It surprised me to see the goddess blush and turn shy.

"Hi, Avery. You look nice."

"Thanks. You, too."

We abandoned the Monopoly game then and moved to the living room while London told us about her experiences at boarding school. Her school was in Switzerland too, but on the other side of the country from Alex's and Hudson's school. I was surprised to learn that they had all seen each other last fall when Alex and Hudson had traveled to London's school for a sports tournament.

The conversation then turned to Anna and Avery, both of whom were going to attend boarding school in the fall. The older kids asked Anna about the school in Austria she had picked, and Anna went on cheerfully and in great detail, talking about things she'd already mentioned to me back when she was deciding which school to attend.

"What about you, Avery?" Hudson asked.

Avery was quiet, staring out the window.

"Avery?"

Avery glanced at Hudson with a blank expression, then she turned her attention to London, who sat across the living room from her. "What?"

"What boarding school are you going to be at?" Hudson asked again.

"TASIS," she said simply.

We all swiveled our heads to look at London.

"Isn't that your school?" Anna asked her.

London didn't answer right away. She was looking back at Avery intently. "Yes," she said finally, almost in a whisper.

"Where's Stacy?" Anna asked.

Anna and I had been the first to arrive at the bleachers that night. She'd had dinner at my house with my parents, and after primping a bit, we walked to the commons.

Avery had just arrived, alone—which was rare— and took a seat next to us. She had that same pensive look that she'd worn since earlier that day when London had shown up at Alex's house.

"Grounded," she said.

"What did she do?" Anna asked.

"Don't know, but her Mom was pissed when I stopped by."

It wasn't uncommon for Stacy to be in trouble with her mom. She felt her mother smothered her, and about once a month it boiled over, and Stacy ended up grounded.

"Oh," I said. "I guess it's just us then. Where do you think the boys and London are?"

Anna let out a little laugh. "Probably at 316, getting sadiki. I wish they'd hurry up."

"Are you really that eager to drink?" I asked.

"Hey, just because you don't want to do it doesn't mean the rest of us can't have a little fun. Besides, what else is there to do?"

"You're not worried that you'll get in trouble?"

"Have I yet? It's not like I get wasted. I just want enough to get buzzed and have some fun. So London still looks like a goddess, huh?"

"Did you expect her not to?" I asked, giving her a look.

"Well, no. I just ... never mind. I'm just being weird."

Avery surprised us by speaking. "I think she looks better. More mature."

Anna let out a little snort. "Well, she's always been mature. At least her body. God, I wish I had boobs like hers."

"It's more than that," Avery said, looking toward the softball field. "She's different."

I wondered if Avery was thinking about how Alex, Hudson, and London seemed to be older now, how they had obviously grown up while at boarding school.

"You think?" Anna asked.

"Isn't it obvious?" Avery said.

"I guess, yeah. They're all different, aren't they? I mean, Hudson and Alex, too. It's like they're almost adults now or something."

"It's different with Alex, though," Avery said, still looking off into the distance.

That caught my attention. "What do you mean?"

She turned to look at me with her unreadable expression. "Something happened to him, I think. Something bad."

Anna and I shared a glance, then she cast her gaze down to her lap. "Yeah. I think something did, too."

I didn't say anything.

It wasn't much later when we saw Hudson, Alex,

and London walking toward us from the pool entrance by the snack bar. Hudson walked ahead of the others like he was leading them. Alex and London walked side by side, their hands almost touching. She seemed happy about something, but Alex had that same defeated look that I was sadly beginning to get used to.

All three of them had bottles of Mirinda.

It became obvious that they'd been drinking when they sat with us. Their faces were rosy, and Alex's eyes were glassed over.

Alex walked up the bleachers in silence and sat on the highest one, his face drawn and pensive.

"Where's Stacy?" Hudson asked.

"Grounded," we all said.

Anna stood and made her way over to sit by Hudson. "Gimme," she said, gesturing to his bottle. He offered it, and she took several swallows. She grimaced comically, then handed the bottle back.

Then Avery did something that shocked us all. She stood and moved closer to us, sitting down next to London.

"I want some," she said, holding out her hand to London.

Everyone's eyes went wide.

"Seriously?" I asked. Was I now going to be the only loser who didn't drink? I'd been okay knowing that there was at least one other person who didn't drink. Avery had been my non-drinking buddy, someone I could feel solidarity with. But now I was the lone dork, the goody-two-shoes who was too scared to join the big kids.

I didn't want to be the only one who didn't drink. I felt kind of betrayed.

London looked like she had no idea what to do. "Oh. Well, um, okay. Here."

Avery took the bottle then looked at it silently.

"It's really nasty shit," Hudson said to her. "It's best to just take big swallows and get it over with. The fewer times you have to drink it the better."

Avery nodded in understanding, then after studying the bottle for a few seconds, brought it to her mouth, tilted her head back, and drank.

She managed one big gulp, then coughed up what she hadn't swallowed, the liquid dribbling down her chin.

"Oh god," she wheezed. "That's horrible." She was shaking her head, and her eyes were screwed shut.

Alex laughed out loud, and Hudson smacked him across the chest. "Don't laugh, jackass. At least she didn't throw up like you did your first time."

That shut Alex up.

"Are you okay?" London asked Avery. She had her hand stretched out like she was going to touch Avery's shoulder, but she pulled it away. "You don't have to have any more."

Avery shook her head, then took another deep drink. She seemed to be better prepared this time, and only hung her head and shuddered.

London seemed to come to some sort of decision, and put her hand on Avery's shoulder, rubbing it. "That's enough," she said. "You don't want to overdo it your first time."

"I give it twenty minutes," Alex said, taking a sip of his own drink.

"What do you mean?" I asked.

He nodded toward Avery. "She's going to be all loopy."

Alex wasn't wrong.

It wasn't long before Avery developed an uncharacteristically dopey look on her face, and she grinned stupidly at us.

Then, when Hudson made a rude joke about a girl he knew at boarding school and her ability to do interesting things with her mouth and bananas, Avery snorted a laugh and nearly toppled over.

"Told you," Alex said to no one in particular.

Avery was drunk, but she seemed to be having a good time. So why shouldn't I be doing it too? They were all kidding around, having fun. Was that such a bad thing?

"More," Avery blurted out after another snort of laughter, but London kept her bottle from Avery.

"Nope. You've had enough."

Avery returned London's look, then got very quiet. She stared at London for a few seconds, then reached out and gently cupped her face.

London was so surprised she visibly flinched, her

mouth a surprised O.

They stared at each other as the rest of us watched them. Then, Avery tilted her head back, and she burst out laughing.

Hudson and Anna joined in the laughter, and I made a soft laugh. Even Alex chuckled.

But not London. She regarded Avery with wonder, her hand moving to touch her own cheek.

For the next hour, we talked about whatever came to mind, easily and fluidly. Alex and Hudson went to the snack bar at one point and came back out with a paper plate of fries that they shared with us.

Avery stood. "I have to pee," she said, swaying as she righted herself.

London immediately jumped up and put her arm around Avery's waist. "Careful."

"I have to pee," she said suddenly and stood, wobbling a bit.

London immediately jumped up and put her arm around Avery's waist. "Careful."

Avery let herself be guided down the bleachers to the ground, and London let her go. She watched as Avery stumbled toward the girls' locker room. Then, after a few moments, London muttered, "Fuck it," and strode purposefully to catch up with Avery. She stopped Avery and said something to her that I couldn't hear. Avery nodded. Then London reached down and took Avery's hand in hers and led her off to the locker room.

Anna, Hudson, and Alex had been talking while this had happened, so they hadn't noticed. I kept my mouth shut.

After about fifteen minutes, Anna came to sit by me, leaving Hudson and Alex on the top seat of the bleachers. "Geez, how long does it take her to pee?"

"Maybe she's sick," I suggested.

"Maybe."

Ten minutes later, London and Avery rejoined us. They were both quiet and subdued. London came to sit by Hudson and Alex, looking troubled, while Avery veered off to the side to sit by herself. She stared out into the night, her face bearing the same expressionless mask that I'd grown used to over the last year.

Over the next week, we settled into our usual pattern. Each day, in the late morning, I'd go to Alex's house to wake him up. Sometimes he woke up without prodding, but sometimes he was clearly hungover, and it took him a few moments to fully wake up. While he showered, I'd do his chores. It wasn't that I felt like I had to do them. I just liked doing something for Alex, like a daily gift to him from me. And it gave me something to do while I waited for him to get ready. He always seemed surprised and thanked me.

Each morning, I watched him when he came out from his room to judge his mood. I kept hoping that he'd come out smiling, his eyes bright, just like I remembered from the previous summer, but he never did. His eyes were flat, emotionless, and he often looked tired.

I'd sigh and try to hide my disappointment.

Alex and I would then head to the pool to meet everyone else. We were always the last to arrive. We'd spend most of the day at the pool, laying out and swimming. The first two days were different because Stacy was still grounded so we didn't see her. Avery sat off to the side, keeping to herself mostly, but she joined us when we had lunch. She and London didn't say anything to each other. For her part, London spent most of her time with Hudson, Anna and myself. When we got into the pool to cool off, Avery would join us, but Alex usually didn't.

At night, we would gather somewhere in the commons—usually the bleachers or playground—and hang out. Hudson and London didn't always have a bottle with them, but Alex always did. I was beginning to see that he drank every night.

Some nights, Alex and Stacy would head off together, and it always made me jealous imagining what they would be doing together.

Avery drank once more that week, something that seemed to delight Stacy, but she didn't get as drunk as she did her first time. Like usual, Avery kept quiet, only speaking when spoken to, but one night when London said she had to go to the bathroom, Avery watched her for a while, then walked off, following her.

After a few moments, I decided I needed to pee too.

"Going to the bathroom," I told Anna.

"Duly noted. You have our permission."

"Smart ass."

"Why do girls always have to go to the bathroom in packs?" Alex wondered aloud.

"Because we're wondrous, mysterious creatures beyond the capability of simple boys to understand," Anna replied, and Hudson laughed.

I walked off, smiling.

The closest bathroom was in the rec hall, which served as the central entertainment hub of the commons. To get to it from the playground, you had to walk down an alley between the bowling alley and the racquetball court building.

I knew that's where London and Avery had gone, so I followed after. Just before I made the turn behind the racquetball court building that led to the rec hall side door—which was in a secluded side alley—I heard Avery's voice.

"London, we need to talk about the kiss."

hat?

I knew it was wrong for me to listen. I should have walked away and left them to their private conversation. But instead, I pushed myself flat against the racquetball court building, just out of sight, and breathed as quietly as I could.

"I shouldn't have kissed you back," Avery went on. "I was just surprised. And a little drunk." There was a moment of silence. "Look, London. I know you've always liked me. I've always known. And I won't lie to you and tell you I'm not flattered by that, because I am. But I don't think I can give you what you want. I'm not sure I feel the same way you do. I don't think we should be alone together anymore."

"But I'm so in love with you," London said, her voice small. "Can't we just try? I know you feel the same way. I see the way you look at me now."

"I'm sorry," Avery replied. "I'm just not ready. I don't know that I'll ever be. This is the way it has to be."

There was a moment of silence, then I heard footsteps coming toward me.

Crap!

I practically dove behind a bush, hoping that it was dark enough that I wouldn't be noticed.

Avery walked past the bush where I was hiding, heading back toward the playground.

I waited for a few seconds, then rounded the corner to see London open the door to the rec hall and step inside. I followed after her.

Once I was in the building, and in the main hall, I saw London slip into the movie room, which was a sort of lounge where we sometimes watched movies.

When I approached, I saw that the lights inside were turned off. I stepped closer and heard the soft sounds of London crying within.

I stepped into the room and closed the door behind me.

"London?" I couldn't see her—it was too dark—but I heard her make a small gasp.

"Chloe?"

As my eyes adjusted to the dark, I saw her sitting on one of the sofas. "Are you okay?" I asked and moved closer.

"Um ... no, not really. Did you hear all that?"

"Yes."

She looked up at me, her eyes defiant like she was expecting the worst. "Do you hate me now? Do you think I'm disgusting?"

I was kind of shocked. I knew that gay people existed—of course, I did—it was just that I never expected that I would know one. Was I disgusted? No. I mean, *I* would never want to kiss a girl—the thought of it made me a little bit uncomfortable—but it didn't bother me if other girls wanted to kiss each other. I shook my head and moved closer to her. "No, of course not. Why would I think that?"

"Because I like girls."

And I suddenly realized why there'd never been any sexual tension between her and Alex, and why she'd never been threatened by his relationship with Stacy. She didn't see him that way because she was gay.

"I don't care about that, London. Can I sit with you?"

"Oh," she said, seeming to relax. "Well ... I guess."

"Do you want to talk about it?" I asked gently once I was sitting next to her.

"What's to talk about? I'm in love with her. She doesn't love me. It's pretty simple."

"How long have you been in love with her?"

"Since I first met her, I guess," she answered. "She's just so ... she has this quiet strength, you know? And she's so caring. I don't know. I guess I've always loved her." London leaned back against the cushions and rubbed at her eyes with her palms.

"So what happened?"

"You mean the kiss?"

"Yeah."

"Well ... she's been different since I came back. Something ... I don't know. She looks at me differently now. Then the other night when she got drunk ... the way she looked at me ... I guess I thought that maybe she liked me. And in the locker room, I *knew* she wanted me to kiss her. So I did. And she kissed me back. But then she kind of freaked out and told me I shouldn't have kissed her. That she didn't like me that way."

I thought about this, trying to wrap my head around this new, unexpected development. "Maybe she's scared."

"Maybe." London let out a big, sad sigh. "It doesn't matter, though. You heard her. She totally rejected me."

"I'm sorry," I said. "Um, does Alex know? About you liking girls, I mean."

She nodded, smiling. "Yes. He's the only person who knows. Well, now you and Avery do, but he's the only person I've come out to."

Now it made sense why London and Alex were so close, and why London seemed to love him so much. She'd bared her soul to him, and he'd accepted her, without condition.

"Don't give up," I told London. "Maybe she just needs to work things out."

"You think?"

"I do. Give her a chance."

"Okay." She straightened, took in a breath, let it out and rubbed at her eyes again. "You're not going to tell anyone, are you?"

"Of course not."

"Not even Anna?"

"I won't tell anyone," I said. "I promise."

CHAPTER FOURTEEN

The next morning, when I let myself into Alex's house, I was surprised to find him already awake, eating cereal at the dining room table.

"Alex. What are you doing up? It's not even eleven."

"Just kind of woke up." He looked up at me, his eyes were red and puffy, and he looked really tired. Then I noticed he was wearing the same clothes as last night.

"Alex, did you not go to sleep last night?"

He shrugged. "No."

"Why not?"

"I didn't want to have dreams."

"Are you okay?" As soon as I said it, I realized what a stupid question it was. Of course, he wasn't okay. He hadn't been okay since he came back from boarding school. And today he seemed to be worse than usual.

He shrugged again. "Not really."

"You should shower. You'll feel better."

He didn't answer.

I stepped close to him, grabbed his arm, and pulled him up from his chair. "Come on. Go shower. I'll clean up."

"Okay. Thanks. I really appreciate you doing my chores."

"It's okay. I don't mind."

Alex's mood hadn't improved when he came back from his shower and changing. I noticed that he was wearing regular shorts.

"You're not in your trunks," I pointed out when he joined me in the living room as if he wasn't already aware. "Do you not want to go to the pool?"

"No. I ... I just want to stay in. With you."

"Okay," I said, then walked over to stand in front of him. "What did you want to do?"

He didn't answer, just looked at me with an intense expression, holding me with his blue eyes. My breath caught, and I couldn't look away.

He stepped close, wrapped his arms around me tightly, and crushed me to him. I was so surprised, I gasped. "I'm so glad I have you," he breathed, his voice husky. "I don't know what I'd do without you."

I wasn't sure what he meant, so I said nothing. I lifted my arms from where they'd been hanging uselessly by my side, and I hugged him back. "It's okay, Alex. I'm here with you. I won't leave you."

He pulled away from me then, but he kept his

hands on my shoulders, looking at me with ... longing? His eyes probed mine, and he licked his top lip with the tip of his tongue. His eyes dropped, and I could tell he was looking at my mouth.

My breath hitched. Was he going to kiss me?

I kept my eyes on his as I parted my lips, waiting to see what he would do.

"I ... ," he said, then stopped.

"You what?"

He shook his head as if clearing a thought away, then stepped away from me. I immediately felt the loss of his presence. "Nothing," he said. "Can we watch a movie? Have you seen *Legend*?"

"No," I said. "Is it good?"

"Yeah. It has some scenes I like."

As Alex worked the Beta-Max, putting the movie in, I sat on the sofa and made myself comfortable.

I could hardly believe it when Alex came over, sat beside me and leaned down, putting his head on my lap.

Why was he being so affectionate with me?

I placed one hand on the side of his head and the other on his upper arm.

I could feel his body heat, smell his intoxicating scent, and I desperately wanted to feel his skin. It was all I could do to concentrate on the movie once it started. I just sat, not sure what to do.

Not even twenty minutes later, Alex reached up with his free hand and grabbed mine, lacing our fingers together. He squeezed tightly.

Instinctively, I squeezed back and found myself stroking his hair with my other hand.

What is going on?

The way he was acting, the casual way he was showing his affection—it was almost like he didn't seem to realize what he was doing.

But I certainly wasn't complaining. How many times over the past nine months had I fantasized about this kind of thing happening? How many times had I dreamed of Alex being this way with me?

I didn't want to ruin this magical moment so I returned his affection as best I could.

It was so sweet.

I wasn't sure how far into the movie we were—maybe an hour in—when I noticed that Alex's eyes were closed and he was breathing deeply.

He'd fallen asleep.

On my lap.

Holding my hand.

I watched him sleep, noting the peaceful expression on his face. Seeing him that way, without the pain tightening his features, tugged at my heart and made my eyes tear up.

He needed me.

And as happy as that made me, it was tempered by confusion.

I didn't know what this all meant.

I'd been totally surprised at first, of course. I mean,

Alex had never shown that type of affection toward me. In fact, I'd never seen him be affectionate like that with anyone, not even London. He certainly wasn't that way with Stacy.

But the way he was being with me, the desperate way he'd clung to me, it was so incredibly intimate.

Was he trying to tell me something? That he liked me? That he was interested in me?

That thrilled me and annoyed me at the same time. On the one hand, I'd been dreaming of Alex thinking of me that way for months. But on the other, his continued casual relationship with Stacy really bothered me. I didn't know where I stood with him if he was involved with Stacy that way.

I pushed those thoughts aside.

Alex had wanted to be alone with me. He'd been affectionate with me. And, possibly, he was interested in me.

I wasn't going to ruin all that by overthinking things.

Someone knocked on the door, which woke Alex, and he sat up, looking confused.

"I'll get that," I said.

When I answered the door, Anna was standing there. I stepped out onto the patio and shut the door behind me.

"Have you been here all morning?" she asked.

"Yes."

"Is he okay?"

"Yes."

"Why do you look so pleased? What happened?"

I leaned in close, even though I knew there was no one around to overhear. "We watched a movie. He fell asleep on my lap."

Her eyes widened. "No!"

"And he's being very sweet. We held hands."

"Get out! Oh my god! Did he try to kiss you?"

Maybe?

I motioned for her to keep it down. "No. And be quiet. He's going to hear you."

"Do you think he likes you?"

I wasn't sure how to answer that. "Maybe?"

"Oh my god!"

"Shhh!"

"Sorry," she said, grinning. "This is just so exciting. Are you going to kiss him?"

"No! Maybe. I don't know. He's with Stacy."

"Oh, please. He's not interested in Stacy. They just mess around."

I scoffed at her. "And you don't see that as a problem? I don't want to share him with her."

"Well, maybe he broke up with her. Or, you know, told her they couldn't mess around anymore."

"Yeah, well, I'm not going to do anything until I know for sure."

Her eyes lit up. "Do you want me to ask Stacy about it?"

"No! Will you settle down? She'll just get pissed off

if she isn't already. You know how she is."

"Yeah, you're right. So what are you going to do?"

"I'm going to go back inside and see what he wants to do. I think he just wants to stay inside. I'm going to hang out with him."

"But no kissing," she said, disappointed.

"No kissing."

"Okay, I'll get out of your hair. But I want details later!"

Back inside, I found Alex waiting for me, still sitting on the sofa.

"Was that Anna?" he asked.

"Yeah. She was just checking up on me."

"Do you want to go out with her?"

"Do you want me to?"

He stood, his gaze lingering on me. "No. I ... will you stay with me? I just want to be alone with you."

"Of course," I said, feeling elated that he wanted to be with me. "Did you want to do something?"

"Can we play a game? Dungeon maybe?"

"That sounds great."

Alex and I played two rounds of Dungeon I won the first game, he the second . I could tell that he simply wanted to do something that would distract him from his pain, and I was happy to go along with it. I did my best to talk about the game, trying to keep his focus on what we were doing.

"I'm kind of hungry," he said when we'd finished the second game. "Do you want sandwiches?"

"Sure. That would be nice."

We made sandwiches together then ate at the table.

When we were done, I told Alex to wait for me in the living room while I cleaned up.

When I was finished, I found him sitting on the sofa, leaning back on the cushion, looking so hurt and lost that it made my own heart hurt for him. He was in so much pain, and I wanted to make it my own, to ease his burden.

I walked up and stood in front of him. His gaze was fixed on his lap.

"Alex."

He looked up at me, his eyes wet. Then two tears tracked down his face, and he took in a shuddering breath.

"Oh, Alex." I knelt in front of him, nudged his knees apart, and leaned into him, taking his hands in mine. "There was nothing you could do. It wasn't your fault."

A short, bitter laugh escaped his lips. "You don't know what you're talking about," he said. "You weren't there."

"I'm sorry you had to go through that, Alex. And I'm sorry you're in so much pain. But you need to realize that it was out of your hands. It was an accident."

"You just don't ... "

"I don't what?"

"Never mind."

163

I didn't know what else to say, but I could sense he needed me, so I leaned into him and rested my head on his chest. His arms came around me, and he held me tight. I could feel his body trembling as he tried not to break down, and I could hear his heart hammering in his chest.

We spent the rest of the afternoon together, playing games and watching old music videos. When it was time for me to leave, he walked me to the door.

"Thank you," he said. "For being with me today."

"It's okay, Alex. I'll be with you whenever you need me. I'll be over every morning, and if you just want to stay in, I'll stay with you. I won't leave you."

I walked home with a sense of elation, wonder, and sadness.

That night, Hudson and London showed up at the bleachers without Alex. When we asked them where he was, they shared a look. "He wanted to be alone," Hudson said. "I'm not sure where he went."

We didn't see Alex at all that night.

CHAPTER FIFTEEN

I went to Alex's house the next morning, as usual, to wake him up.

I found him in his room, asleep in his bed, the sheet tangled together with his legs.

I nudged him. "Alex. It's time to wake up."

"Nnnhh," he mumbled, then opened his eyes. "What time is it?"

"Ten thirty. Come on, get up and take a shower."

He rolled over on his back, and when I saw that he was naked and had an erection, I spun around. "I'll wait for you up front." I fled his room, blushing furiously.

When he came out, I was happy to see that he appeared to be in a much better mood than the day before.

Holy crap He's smiling

He held a one-liter bottle half-full of a clear liquid. "What's that?" I asked.

"Sadiki."

"You're going to start drinking? It's not even noon yet."

"So? I was just going to have a little bit."

I was annoyed. Everyone was drinking except me. It made me feel like an outsider, like I'd been left behind. I didn't like that. I didn't want to be the loser looking in and not being part of the fun. And I was tired of enforcing some value that I wasn't even sure I believed in anymore.

I considered.

It was early. I didn't have to be home for seven hours. That was plenty of time for me to get a little drunk and then sober up. I could just stay here with Alex, alone, so there was no chance of getting caught by a random adult.

It was safe.

I nodded to myself, ready to take the plunge.

"Can I have some?" I asked.

Alex raised an eyebrow. "Seriously? You want a drink?"

"Yeah," I said, feeling a bit defensive. "Is that not okay?"

"No, no. That's fine. I'm just surprised. Wait for me at the dining table. I'll get the Mirinda.

He joined me a few minutes later, loaded up with four glasses. He placed two in front of me, then put a little bit of sadiki in one and filled the other with Mirinda. He did the same for himself, then went back to the kitchen. He returned a moment later with another glass filled with ice.

"Okay," he said. "This is going to be the harshest thing you've ever tasted. It's basically moonshine. You could run an engine on it. It's going to be horrible. Understood?"

I nodded, remembering how Avery had reacted to her first drink.

"So what you're going to do is have some sadiki and swallow it as fast as you can. Then you chase it down with Mirinda, as much as it takes to wash out the sadiki. Then you'll want to suck on an ice cube. Okay?"

I nodded again. "Yeah, okay."

"Are you ready?"

"Yes," I said, grabbing the glass of sadiki. Then before I could think about it, I took a healthy drink.

I nearly coughed it out, but controlled myself and swallowed, feeling it burn its way down to my stomach. I grabbed the glass of Mirinda next and drank greedily.

"Oh my god," I managed. "That is disgusting." I thought about how he, Hudson and London drank casually from their bottles throughout the nights, wondering how they could take it. I guess they were used to it.

Alex chuckled. "Told you. Now do that a few more times, as quick as you can. It's better to just get it over with."

I drank twice more, each time taking in a little bit more sadiki.

"Okay," Alex said, taking my glass of sadiki away. I realized he'd already finished his. "That's enough. Let's sit down."

I could feel it as soon as I stood up. There seemed to be a blanket of heavy air over everything, and when I turned my head, everything took a second to shift with me. I felt flushed, but in a good way, and a very nice sensation ran through me like a current.

"Holy bananas. I think I'm drunk." For some reason, that made me giggle.

Alex smiled, grabbed my arm and pulled me along. "Come on."

He led me to the middle of the living room, in front of the TV, and we sat down on the floor, cross-legged, facing each other.

"Are you okay?"

"Yes! I feel really ... "

"Good?"

"Yes!" It was more than that, though. I could feel the worry over Alex, and my self-doubt lift away, and I felt free, like all the things that had been holding me back from expressing myself had vanished.

A little laugh escaped me, and Alex chuckled in return. Which made me laugh more. Realizing I wasn't even sure what I was laughing at seemed so ridiculous, a fit of giggles came over me.

"What are you laughing at?"

"I don't know!"

When I settled down, I looked over at Alex who was regarding me with amusement.

I stared at him in wonder.

Oh my gosh, he's so beautiful

I couldn't look away. In fact, I was looking at him with an intensity I'd never felt before. I felt a powerful pull, an attraction that I couldn't escape.

Before I even knew what was happening, I was on my hands and knees, moving toward him. I paused when my face was just inches from his.

He was watching me, waiting.

I licked my lips, then leaned forward until our lips were touching.

It was like sparks exploded in my body, and I could feel a bolt of excitement shoot right through me. I moved my lips against his, and my excitement grew when I felt him kiss me back. This amazing feeling filled me then, an exhilaration that was so powerful it seemed to take me over. I leaned closer in, pressing against Alex, and I probed his lips with my tongue. He opened his mouth and I felt his tongue touch mine. I felt my body react as my arousal grew.

And then suddenly I realized what I was doing, and I sat back down, feeling both amazing and shy. I was unable to meet his gaze. "I, um ... what are we going to do now?" I asked, hoping he'd just forget that I kissed him.

"I don't know," he said after a few seconds, his eyes

still looking back at me enticingly. "We probably shouldn't go to the pool. The sun might make you sick. It takes some getting used to. And you might get in trouble."

"Can we just stay here?"

"Yeah, sure. What did you want to do?"

"Can we just talk?"

And no kissing!

"Okay."

"So ... " I began, not sure what to say. Then a random thought struck me. "I played D&D."

That caught his attention. "Oh yeah?"

"Yeah. I played with Ryan and Anna and his little brother. Sean, too." Sean was one of the kids who hadn't been here last summer when Alex was around, but I knew they knew each other.

"Cool," he said. "How did you like it?"

"It was fun. The rules were intimidating at first, but I got the hang of it. It was cool to make characters. I think that was my favorite part."

Then we fell silent and just watched each other. His eyes never left mine, but I was too shy to keep mine on his face for too long. I had to look away. But when I glanced back at him, he was still looking at me.

"What?" I finally managed say, feeling like maybe there was something on my face.

He didn't answer right away, just kept looking at me. Just as I was about to look away gain, he spoke. "You're ..."

I could see his eyes roaming over my face.

"I'm what?"

"You're beautiful."

Holy crap!

I just stared back at him, amazed that he'd said that to me.

"You're so beautiful," he said again, then finally looked away, his cheeks coloring.

I didn't say anything. I couldn't. I was too stunned. I just sat there staring back at him like an idiot.

Then he stood up and held out a hand to me. "Let's watch something."

Still somewhat in a daze, I let him help me up. He turned on the TV which was showing old music videos, and he led me to the sofa where we sat close together in silence.

I was so happy I thought I might die.

The next day we had lunch under the pavilion at the pool.

"I have an idea," Alex said, looking off toward the pool as he grabbed some fries from his plate.

I'd gone to Alex's house earlier to wake him up, and I'd found him in an expressionless mood, his eyes dark and full of pain. I wanted him to get out and be around our friends, so I dragged him to the pool where we met everyone else.

"Oh yeah? Hudson said. "Are you going to share

with the rest of the class?"

Alex swiveled his head to Hudson. "Let's go to the hills."

"The hills?" I asked. "You mean the hills behind the compound?" A few kilometers to the west of the compound were some small hills that marked the beginning of the badlands that stretched west toward the Red Sea for a few hundred miles. I'd never been, and as far I knew neither had Anna, Stacy, or Avery. "Isn't that dangerous?"

"It can be," Alex said. "But I think it will be okay."

"I'll go," Anna put in, then gave me an apologetic look when I didn't say anything.

"Are you sure?" London asked. "I don't know."

"We're in," Stacy said, and Avery nodded.

"Won't we get in trouble?" I asked.

Alex let out a small laugh. "Don't worry. I doubt anyone will even notice. We'll only be gone for a few hours."

"Okay," London said. "But just for a few hours. I need to be back for dinner."

Everyone turned to look at me.

Remembering my resolve to not be the boring kid that sat out while everyone else had fun, I nodded. "Okay."

Alex stood. "Good. You girls go home and get dressed up as much like a boy as you can. Put your hair up under caps."

"What? Why?" I asked.

"Because we might run into Arabs, and they might get weird if they think you're girls."

"But we are girls," I pointed out.

"Yes, and that's why you need to dress like a boy. If they think we're all boys from a distance, they'll leave us alone." Then he looked at London. "You're going to have to do something about your boobs."

London blushed and covered her chest with her arms. "What?"

"Can you flatten them out somehow?"

"Are you being serious?"

"Well, it's pretty obvious you're a girl, even from a distance, with them sticking out like they do."

London's blush deepened. "I could wear my racer underneath my clothes, I guess," she said.

"Okay," Alex said. "We'll meet at Anna's house in half an hour."

With that, Alex threw his plates away in the trash, grabbed his stuff, and walked off with Hudson.

"I look ridiculous," I said as we walked up the street through camp three to the west end of the compound. I was wearing jeans, a loose T-shirt, and had my hair up, covered with a stupid-looking ball-cap. With my shades on I probably actually did look like a boy.

At least I wasn't alone. The other girls were similarly dressed and looked kind of dorky, too. Except for London, who even with her loose clothing, slightly flattened boobs the racer hadn't really helped that much , and hair under a cap, still looked sexy.

"It's not just you," Stacy said, looking as put out as I felt. "And it's hot in these jeans."

"Stop complaining," Anna said. "Did you just want to hang out at the compound and do nothing? At least we're doing something different."

A few minutes later we arrived at the west wall. The boys climbed up, straddled the wall, then helped the girls over. As I was flipping my legs over the wall, I was sure everyone in the compound was watching us, but when I nervously looked around at the long row of houses, I didn't see a single person.

Once the boys joined us on the other side of the wall, we headed toward the hills in the west. The terrain was flat and gravelly, and there were almost no trees that we could see between us and the hills.

We walked.

"It will take us about thirty minutes," Hudson explained. "If we keep our pace up."

"This seems dangerous," I said, still feeling nervous.

"Don't worry," Alex said over his shoulder from where he led. "It used to be, but not really anymore."

"What do you mean 'used to be'?" I asked.

"There used to be packs of wild dogs and baboons."

"Seriously?" I looked around, expecting to see a horde of dogs bearing down on us.

"Yeah. We had to deal with them a few times."

"Holy crap. What did you do?"

Hudson chuckled. "Ran like hell to the boulders. We climbed up to where the dogs couldn't reach us and waited them out."

That seemed crazy to me. "Jesus. They could have torn you to pieces."

"Probably," Alex said. "But that was a really long time ago. We haven't seen any dogs for years. We'll be okay."

"What about the baboons?" Anna asked, looking nervous too. "I hear they can be dangerous."

"We saw a pack once," Hudson said, "when we went back into the hills, but they were one hill over and ignored us."

"If we're going to run into any animals," Alex said, "it'll probably be goats. And the only dangerous thing they do is fart."

A snort of laughter escaped Stacy. "That's just great."

We walked on. Alex and Hudson took the lead, with London behind them. Stacy and Avery followed after, and Anna and I trailed behind.

"So are you going to tell me why you've had a stupid grin on your face since yesterday?" Anna asked, leaning in.

Did I really want to tell her? I'd been keeping it to myself because, honestly, I was embarrassed.

"I drank with Alex yesterday."

I heard Anna take in air. "You drank?"

"Yep."

"Oh, man, I so wish I could have seen that. And you were alone with Alex?"

I didn't say anything.

"You're blushing," she said excitedly. "Why are you blushing? Something happened, didn't it? Oh my god! Tell me, tell me, tell me!"

"Will you settle down? I don't want the rest to hear."

"Okay, okay. But you're killing me. Please tell me."

I sighed heavily. "I kissed Alex."

"No. Way."

"Yes, way."

"When you were drinking? How much did you have?"

"Enough, I guess," I said, shrugging. "It was crazy. It was like I couldn't control myself. I was doing it before I could even think about it."

"Did he kiss you back?"

Did he ever "Yes."

"And?"

"And what?"

"Geez! How was it?"

I kept quiet, feeling heat creep up my neck, and suddenly my cheeks were flaming. "It was amazing."

"Better than Ryan?"

It was a little bit unfair to compare Ryan to Alex. Ryan had been a decent kisser, and, at first, kissing him had been fun. But I didn't love Ryan. I wasn't even all that attracted to him. With Alex, on the other hand, there'd been fireworks, explosions of desire, and I'd felt like I could get lost in his lips forever.

"No comparison," I said. "I wanted to rip his clothes off."

"Did you?"

"No! I told you. I'm not going to do anything like that when he's ... " I leaned in close, whispering in her ear. "When he's doing stuff with Stacy. I'm not going to share him."

"So are you going to go after him? If you ask him out, I'm sure he'll dump Stacy."

"I don't know," I said. "It's complicated. There's other stuff going on."

"The stuff you can't tell me about?"

"Yes."

"Well, I still think—"

Alex and Hudson had stopped, holding their arms back toward us girls, their palms out, telling us to stop.

It got very quiet.

We were by a lone tree, partially under its sparse shade, and up ahead, about a hundred feet was a jumble of large granite boulders. It looked like we were about halfway to the hills.

"Oh god," London said suddenly, holding her hand over her mouth and nose. "What is that?"

And then Stacy and Avery stepped back, turning around, covering their mouths.

"What is it?" I asked, stepping forward with Anna.

Then it practically slapped me in the face. There was a horrid, putrid stench in the air. I'd never smelled anything like it before, and I hoped I never would again.

"Jesus," Anna said, nearly gagging. "What is that?"

"Stay here," Alex said, and he and Hudson approached the pile of boulders. Then they hopped up on the lower rocks and looked down into the pile. They had their hands over their mouths and noses, too.

They came back to us a few seconds later. "It's a dead camel," Alex said.

"Really?" Anna asked.

And then Avery was walking toward the boulders.

"What are you doing?" Stacy called after her.

"I want to see," Avery replied.

Stacy hesitated, cursed under her breath, then followed after her.

"Do you want to see?" Anna asked.

"No! That's disgusting. Why would I want to see a dead camel?"

"Aren't you curious?"

"No! I can barely stand the stench from here."

"I'm going to look," she said.

"Are you crazy? Why would you want to do that?"

She shrugged. "I'm curious, I guess."

"You go ahead then. I'm staying right here."

London had moved closer to us. "Are you going to see?"

"No," I replied as Anna walked toward the boulders.

"Me neither," London said. "That smells so bad."

When Avery, Stacy, and Anna returned, they all looked pale, especially Anna.

"Are you okay?" I asked her.

"I wish you'd talked me out of that."

"Can we please leave?" London asked.

"Yeah, let's get the hell out of here," Hudson said.

So we walked back until we couldn't smell the dead camel anymore, and made a wide arc around the boulders.

When we'd left the dead camel far behind us, I began to study the hills up ahead, which were much closer now and looming larger than I'd expected. At the base of the hill we were hiking toward lay a heap of huge boulders piled on top of and against each other.

"Is that where we're going?" I asked, raising my voice so the boys could hear.

"The boulders, yeah," Alex called back.

It only took ten more minutes to reach the boulders. They were huge. The biggest were larger than houses, and even the smallest were several times the size of a car.

They all lay together on a base of flat granite, like a big plate on which the boulders were served.

Alex and Hudson lead us into the pile, huge rocks on either side of us. They stopped at one of the smallest. It leaned against a larger boulder.

Alex turned around and pointed up. "We're going up there." I turned around to look. What was probably the largest boulder, twice the size of a house, loomed over us.

"Follow us," Hudson said, then he and Alex jumped up on the smallest boulder.

We followed.

CHAPTER SIXTEEN

The boys led us from one boulder to another, each larger than the last. Sometimes we had to jump from one rock to another, sometimes we had to scramble up on our hands and knees, but eventually we found ourselves standing on top of the largest boulder.

We were easily sixty feet up.

Alex and Hudson sat down, facing back towards the compound, which was just a dark, thin line in the distance.

"So this is it," Hudson said. "We can hike up to the top of the hill if you guys want, but it's cool if you just want to hang out here."

"This is fine," Anna said, and the other girls agreed.

So we sat, much like we did on the bleachers, and a silence settled over us.

"That kind of freaked me out," Anna said from where she sat next to me.

"The camel?" I asked.

"Yes. It was—"

I put up a hand. "I don't want to know."

"It's just ... I've never seen something dead like that. It didn't look like it had been dead long. And it was all bloated and—"

"Anna! Shut up! I don't want to hear it."

"Do you think that happens to people?" Avery asked, and we all turned our attention to her, surprised that she'd spoken at all. "Like if people die in the wilderness and no one finds them."

Oh, Jesus

Hudson and I immediately glanced at Alex, concern etched in both our features.

But Alex just looked off into the distance, seemingly lost in his own thoughts.

"Can we not talk about this?" I said. "I don't want to talk about dead people."

"I saw one once," Avery said.

"A dead person?" Stacy asked.

I was kind of freaking out. I did not want to be talking about dead people in front of Alex.

"Yeah," Avery replied. "On the way to Jeddah. There was an accident. I saw a body on the street."

"Did it freak you out?" Stacy asked.

"No. But I kept thinking, that used to be a person. That used to be someone who had friends and walked around and talked and had thoughts. And now they're just a pile of meat and bones. I was wondering what happened to them after that. Where they went."

"You mean like heaven?" Anna asked.

Avery nodded. "Or whatever."

"You don't believe in heaven?" London asked.

"I don't know," Avery replied. "Something like it, I guess. I mean, there has to be somewhere we go after we die."

"You mean like our souls?" I asked, finding myself being drawn into the conversation.

"Yeah. Our souls. I think our souls go somewhere."

"But what if we go to some sort of hell where we suffer for all eternity?" Anna asked.

"It doesn't matter," Alex said loudly, cutting us all off. "It doesn't matter if it's heaven or hell. You'll remember your past life either way. You'll still remember all the things you've done. You'll suffer either way."

What will you remember, Alex?

We were silent for long moments.

The conversation, thankfully, lightened after that. It started off with us talking about movies, then focused in on *The Hitcher*, a movie about a young guy who picks up an older man, a hitchhiker who turns out to be a psychopathic killer. Anna and Stacy were arguing about who they'd rather have sex with, the young guy or the mature man.

"The young guy, of course!" Stacy said with conviction. "I wouldn't want to be with a creepy old guy."

"Yeah, but the young guy probably wouldn't know

what he was doing," Anna countered. "The mature guy has been around. He knows how to please a woman. He could do things to you the young guy probably wouldn't even know about."

"But he's as old as my dad! Gross!"

"Suit yourself," Anna said. "You'd just be stuck with a guy who would never get you off. I, on the other hand, would be a very happy girl."

I couldn't believe they were discussing this. "I wish you guys would talk about something else."

"What's wrong with talking about sex? It's not like you don't ever talk about it."

I sighed. "Okay, fine. Talk about sex."

Anna looked like she was going to burst with glee. "Okay! How far have you guys gone?"

"What do you mean?" London asked.

"You know," Anna said. "Which base. First? Second? Third?"

"Define the bases for us," Hudson said.

Anna rolled her eyes. "First is French kissing. Second is going up a girl's shirt. Third is going below the belt. And home is sex."

"You go first then," I said. "Since you're so eager to talk about this."

"Fine, I will," she said, looking around at us, suddenly looking less confident. "Second." That surprised me. She'd never told me about that. Then she turned to Avery, whose eyes widened a little. "Avery?"

She looked at each of us, her features flat, then after

a while spoke quietly. "Second."

"Seriously?" Anna asked in a surprised tone. I was surprised as well. Avery had never had a boyfriend as far as I knew. "With who?"

"Tommy," she answered. "Eighth grade."

"Get. Out. You and Tommy?"

"I think we've talked enough about me," Avery said. "It's Stacy's turn."

"Third," Stacy said without preamble. We didn't need to ask who she'd done that with, because Stacy had told Anna and me, and there were more than one, including Alex. "Your turn, Chloe."

"I, um ... " I really didn't want to answer this, mostly because I'd never told anyone, not even Anna. I felt a serious blush creep up my neck and heat my cheeks. "Third."

Anna's eyes widened. "Holy shit. You did? With Ryan? Why didn't you tell me?"

It was all I could do just to nod. "Yeah."

Anna's gave me a stern look. "You and I are going to have a nice, little chat later, young lady." She then turned to London. "Your turn."

London blushed, and she looked kind of panicked. "Um ... I ... " She looked to Avery, who returned her gaze. "First?"

I couldn't believe it. London, the Sex Goddess, had only ever French kissed?

Stacy snorted a laugh like she didn't believe London's words. Given what she believed London and

Alex had done, that wasn't surprising.

"You're kidding," Anna said to London. "First? That's it? With who?"

London's eyes briefly flitted to Avery. "Not telling," she said.

Had London's kiss with Avery been her first? That was somehow ... incredibly sweet.

"You're next, Hudson," Anna said to him, prodding his leg.

"Third," he said simply. "Girl at boarding school."

Then we all turned our attention to Alex, who sat apart from us, throwing little rocks out in front of him. He remained quiet.

"Well?" Anna said impatiently.

Still, Alex didn't answer.

Hudson cleared his throat. "He's just being modest. Alex here has been around the bases several times."

That same jealousy stabbed at me. Alex had already told me that Taylor had been his first, but hearing it again made an irrational anger rise up within me, and I didn't really know how to deal with it.

Stacy didn't look all that pleased, either.

Alex stood. "This is the dumbest conversation I've ever had the pleasure of not being part of. Let's get going. It's getting late."

We met at the bleachers that night, like usual. When Anna and I arrived, Stacy and Avery were already there, drinking milkshakes. About half an hour later, London showed up.

"Where are the boys?" I asked her.

"They're having some sort of video game war. They said they'd be out later."

Alex and Hudson eventually arrived, each of them carrying a bottle of Mirinda. When they sat, Hudson offered his bottle to London and Anna, and they each had a fair amount.

Stacy got up and went to sit next to Alex, leaning in and whispering in his ear. He offered her his bottle, and she had a drink. Then Avery joined them, drinking as well.

My turn, I guess.

I sat next to Anna and held my hand out to Hudson.

He raised an eyebrow in surprise, then handed me the bottle.

I took a drink and fought hard not to spit it out.

Unlike at Alex's house, where the sadiki and Mirinda were in separate glasses, and I could chase the sadiki, the Mirinda in Hudson's bottle was mixed with sadiki, so there was no way to rinse my mouth.

"Gack," was all I could say.

The sadiki burned its way down to my stomach where it settled. A warmth began to spread through my body, eventually reaching my face and making me feel flushed.

It wasn't long before I was buzzed and started feeling really good. We'd remained in our little groups: me, Anna, London and Hudson together, and Alex, Stacy, and Avery sitting off by themselves. Stacy stuck to Alex's side like glue, and her hand stayed firmly on his thigh.

I wanted to slap her.

As I watched, Alex stood.

"Gotta pee," he said and handed his bottle to Stacy. He lumbered down the bleachers, then headed toward the boys' locker room.

Anna stood and held her hand out to me expectantly. "Time to talk," she said.

I grabbed her hand, and she led me to the other side of the bleachers, where we had some privacy.

"Third base, huh?" she said once we got settled. "When?"

I didn't really want to be having this conversation, but I knew Anna wouldn't let it go. I sighed. I'd done it more than once, so I just mentioned the first time. "At the party you had last February. We were making out and it just sort of happened."

"How does that just sort of happen? You have to go through several deliberate steps to get there. Did you do it to him or did he do it to you?"

"We did it to each other."

"And?"

"And what?"

"You're killing me," she said, frustrated. "Did you see it?"

"Yes."

"Was it ... you know ... like Alex?"

I shook my head. "No. It was normal, I guess."

I needed to stop talking about this or I would die from embarrassment. "What about you? You never told me you did that. When? With who?"

Now Anna looked embarrassed, and she put her hands up over her face and peeked out between her fingers at me. "Eighth grade?" she said sheepishly.

"And with whom did you have the honor to do this with?"

She leaned in close and whispered in my ear. "Hudson."

"Hudson?!" I couldn't mask my shock. "You went to second base with—"

"Oh no," Anna said suddenly, a panic in her voice, and she stood. She was looking over my shoulder, out toward the softball field.

I stood and turned to see what she was looking at. "What is it?"

She pointed, and I followed her gaze to the light tower behind left field, up against the east wall of the compound. It was hard to see anything because of the bright lights, but as my eyes acclimated, I saw him.

Alex was climbing up the pole, nearing the top, which had to be nearly a hundred and fifty feet in the air.

I gasped, and a panic seized me. It felt like my heart had fallen into my stomach like a lead ball.

"Alex!" I screamed, then found myself running toward the light tower. I ran faster than I ever had in my life, and I made it to the base of the light tower in seconds.

Alex was still climbing, nearing the small platform at the top.

"Alex!" I shouted again, just as everyone else came running up to me. "Get down!"

I watched him, my heart thundering in my chest.

If he slipped, the fall would kill him. There was no doubt.

I looked to my friends, hoping in vain that one of them could do something, anything, to get Alex back down, but they were just looking up at him, scared expressions on their faces.

"Jesus ... " Anna said hoarsely, "If he falls ... "

We all began shouting and screaming at Alex, begging him to come down, but he either ignored us or didn't hear.

Please, please, please don't fall

Stacy and London were on the verge of tears, and even Hudson looked scared.

Then Alex reached the platform and stopped. He stayed underneath it, still clinging to the ladder, but it was clear he was trying to figure out a way to get on the platform.

By then I was crying, feeling utterly helpless, and

wondering if I was going to witness Alex dying.

I watched, unable to do anything else.

Suddenly, Alex slipped, and he teetered for a second. We all screamed. Then his arm shot out, and he grabbed the bar of the ladder, just as his feet lost purchase.

My heart froze with terror as I watched helplessly, waiting for him to fall. Waiting for him to fall to his death.

Alex hung there, clinging to the ladder with one hand.

Don't let go Please don't let go Please don't die Please

Finally, after several excruciatingly long seconds, he reached out with his other hand and pulled himself onto the ladder.

Anna was with me, holding me, and I saw that she was crying too.

Alex began to descend the light tower, slowly, rung by rung, as we watched helplessly.

When he finally reached the ground, my heart began to unclench. He stepped toward us, a crazed, wild look in his eyes.

"Wow, that was—"

London stepped toward and slapped him across the face so hard that Alex stumbled to the side, a bright red mark on his face. He looked back at her like he couldn't understand what she was so upset about.

Then Hudson was there, and he grabbed Alex by

the shirt and slammed him hard against the concrete wall. "What the fuck is wrong with you?" he shouted. "Killing yourself isn't going to bring her back!"

Alex shoved Hudson back. "You have no idea what you're talking about! So keep your fucking mouth shut and leave me the fuck alone!"

"So you can keep doing stupid shit like this? Look at the girls, you jackass! Look at them! You scared them! What if you'd fallen? Do you know what it would be like for them to see you die?"

It was too late.

The words had come out.

Hudson didn't look angry anymore. He looked stricken.

"Alex ... I didn't mean ... I'm sorry."

Alex's face was dark and menacing, and there was a burning rage in his eyes. Then he lashed out, his fist smashing into Hudson's face, sending him sprawling on the ground. Alex just stared down at him, that same untamed look blazing in his eyes. "You weren't there," he spat out. "You didn't watch her die. You didn't walk back to town with her blood all over you. You didn't ..." Alex's face crumpled and tears streamed from his eyes. "You. Weren't. There."

He stepped away from Hudson, then pushed past us.

We were quiet as he walked away. The only sound was our heavy breaths and London's quiet sobs.

As terrified as I was, as angry as I was at Alex for

scaring me so badly, I couldn't get that desperate, hopeless look that had filled his eyes out of my mind. I couldn't see anything other than that terrible pain that came over him.

The anger slowly faded, replaced by a concern so deep it hurt. I realized then that Alex didn't care if he lived or died. His pain was so great that he was willing to gamble with his life to make it go away.

We spent the rest of the night sitting quietly on the bleachers. Avery held Stacy, soothing her, while Anna stayed close to me, both seeking and wanting to give comfort. London tended to Hudson, making him hold a bag of ice to his cheek which had swollen and turned an ugly red.

We sat together, but I think we all felt alone.

CHAPTER SEVENTEEN

"Mom?" The next day, I'd showered and dressed, still feeling tired from a restless night, and walked to the kitchen where Mom was laying out breakfast. "Can I talk to you about something?"

She turned toward me, and when she saw my face, her smile disappeared. "Oh, Jesus," she said, looking panicked. "Please tell me you're not pregnant."

Ever since she had caught me making out with Sam Peterson on my bed, Mom had been super paranoid about me having sex and getting pregnant. And even though she had liked Ryan, whenever he came over, and we hung out in my room—with the door open—Mom still checked on us every half hour. "No, Mom. I'm only fourteen. Of course, I'm not pregnant." The relief on her face was comical, but I didn't smile. "It's about Alex."

"Oh, thank god." She took in a breath and let it out in a rush. "Come sit. We can talk while you

194

eat."

I followed, and I sat, but I didn't eat. I was still freaked out and didn't have much of an appetite.

"What's this about Alex?"

"Mom ... I think there's something wrong with him. I think he wants to hurt himself."

Mom's face instantly turned serious as she went into Concerned Mother mode. "Why do you say that?"

I somehow felt like I was about to betray Alex by sharing his secret, but after last night, after what he'd said, it was pretty easy to piece together an idea of what had happened. Hudson knew. London knew. And I knew that Anna had figured it out because when we'd walked home, she'd asked if Alex had been with someone who had died. I felt bad for not telling her the whole story, but I acknowledged that she'd guessed correctly.

I placed both hands flat on the table to ground myself. Then I told Mom what had happened to Alex's girlfriend, and how he'd been there with her when she'd died. I told her about how different Alex was now, how the life had gone from his eyes, and how he drank almost every night—I could see Mom tick that off in her head for later discussion—and how he'd been so reckless. I told her about the backflip and the light tower. The only things I left out were when I'd found Alex crying, and the day we spent together when I'd taken care of him. That was private, and I wasn't about to share those tender moments with anyone.

When I finished talking, Mom was quiet for a long time.

"Chloe … when a loved one dies, it can be very traumatic. In Alex's case—being with her when she died—I imagine that is devastating. Obviously, Alex is having a hard time dealing with his grief. He doesn't know how to deal with his pain, or the trauma he went through." She reached out and grabbed my hand. "Honey, I think Alex needs help. He needs to see someone."

"Like who?"

"A professional. A psychologist or a therapist."

"But there's no one like that here," I pointed out.

Mom sighed, sounding like she was feeling Alex's pain, too. "No, there isn't. How has his mother been taking this?"

"His mom is in the States with his big sister. It's just him and his dad, and his dad works all the time."

She nodded. "So he's alone much of the time."

"He's with us," I said. "He's with us all day mostly."

"Tell me about the drinking. Where is he getting alcohol?"

Oh boy. I shouldn't have mentioned the drinking. Now Mom was going to dig and dig until she found out everything. "Um … well, Alex and Hudson and London have some alcohol stashed somewhere." I anticipated the next question. "I don't know where," I lied. "They just show up with it sometimes."

Mom gave me *that* look. "Have *you* been drinking?"

I put on the straightest, most convincing face I could. "No, of course not!" I felt bad for telling such a big lie, but I knew that if she found out I'd been drinking I'd be grounded for the rest of the summer, and she'd talk to everyone's parents. They'd all get in trouble, too. It would be a disaster.

"Back to Alex," she said, seemingly convinced of my innocence. "That boy needs help. He needs to talk to someone. I think his father needs to send him back to the States to his mother so he can get help." She gave my hand a squeeze before letting go. "Thank you for trusting me with this, honey. You did the right thing telling me. I'll speak with his father. Now finish your breakfast."

We didn't see Alex for two days. When I went to his house to wake him up, I found his door locked, and when I knocked on his bedroom window, there was no answer.

I didn't stop trying, though.

On the third day after the light tower incident, I

went to Alex's house in the late morning, just like I did every day, and found the front door unlocked, so I went in. Alex was in his bedroom, asleep and tangled in his sheets.

"Alex."

He didn't stir.

"Alex," I said louder, stepping closer.

"Nnnn," was his reply.

I stepped even closer and pressed my hand against his bare shoulder, shaking him gently. "Alex. Wake up."

He lifted his head, peeked up at me.

"Hey, Chloe."

Was that … his voice was light, almost teasing.

"Take a shower," I told him. "I'll do your chores."

Twenty minutes later, Alex walked into the kitchen where I was drying the last of the dishes. His hair was wet and messy, and he wore regular shorts and a tight tank top that showed off his sexy chest and shoulders.

Most surprising, though, was that he appeared to be in a good mood. No. It was more than that. His eyes were clear, free of pain, and I saw a purpose in them.

"You don't have to do that, you know," he said, leaning against the door jamb. "I mean, I'm glad that you do, but you don't have to."

"I know," I said, turning to face him. "I just like

to. Do you want to go to the pool?"

"No. I want to stay here with you. Is that okay?"

Was it? I figured it was okay. Maybe I could get him to talk about the light tower. "Yeah, sure. Movie?"

"Let's play a game."

"Dungeon?"

"Sure."

So that's what we did.

Alex's mood was better than I had seen all summer. He smiled—real smiles that reached his eyes. And his eyes … they were peaceful.

Had he accepted Taylor's death and was trying to move on? Had he accepted that there was nothing he could have done? Something had clearly changed. It was obvious, practically written on his face.

I was hoping that he'd tell me what it was. I was hoping he'd open up to me again.

After we'd finished the second game, Alex said, "I'm hungry. There's leftover chili. I made it myself."

"Really? Sure. Let me help." I stood and joined him in the kitchen. Alex was at the counter, pulling bowls down from the cabinets, and getting out the silverware.

I opened the fridge to take stock.

There wasn't much there, just eggs, milk, some bread, and sodas. The chili was in Tupperware, on the top shelf.

"Chloe."

I straightened and turned around.

Alex was standing in front of me, his hands hanging low at his sides, and his eyes blazed with something primal.

I let the refrigerator door close.

Alex stood there looking at me. Then, in one single motion, he moved toward me and I moved backward until my back hit the refrigerator door and a small breath of air escaped me. Alex lingered, just inches from me, staring into my eyes. I stared back, feeling anxious and excited. Then his eyes lowered as he looked at my mouth, and I looked at his, unable to focus on anything else. Something powerful ran through me when he licked his lips. Slowly, he brought a hand up and caressed my cheek, making my breath hitch in my throat. My heart pounded as he ran his thumb along my lips, causing my knees to go weak.

Then he leaned in, closer and closer, and pressed his lips against mine softly. I didn't respond. I couldn't. I was still too surprised. He pulled back slightly, and his beautiful blue eyes looked directly into mine. They were dark, so full of desire that it made my body react, low in my belly.

He kissed me again.

He was careful and gentle, as if he were waiting for me to let him know that what he was doing was okay. Finally, I was able to move, and I placed my hands around his waist, pulling him closer to me, wanting him to know that I liked what he was doing. I kissed him back. He pressed up against me, reaching behind my neck, and pulled me into him, so there was no space between our bodies. When I opened my mouth, Alex met my tongue with his, and a quiet groan escaped me.

This went beyond anything I'd ever felt before. It was amazing, and it was the most wonderfully arousing thing I'd ever experienced, and I didn't want it to stop, ever.

I wanted more. *Much* more.

I met him with a force that surprised me, and I wrapped my arms around his neck, pulling myself into him, as our tongues danced and our lips moved against each other.

I was lost, falling into my desire, and briefly, I wondered how far this would go, and if I was ready.

His hand moved down to my collarbone, then my shoulder, caressing my skin as he kissed me. I placed my hand on his chest, feeling his muscles under his shirt, and loving the feel of it.

But then his hand moved down, and he cupped my breast. Something snapped inside of me, like a bolt of lightning.

What am I doing?

I wasn't going to do this. I wasn't going to be just another one of Alex's casual encounters. I didn't want to do this if I wasn't with him, if he wasn't mine. My hormones were raging through my body, driving a powerful need for him—for this to go further—but I forced myself to stop.

I put both of my hands on his chest and pushed him away.

"Stop," I said breathlessly.

"What's wrong?" he asked, wiping his mouth with the back of his hand. He was breathing hard, too. "Did I hurt you?"

I stepped to the side, so I wasn't trapped between him and the refrigerator. "No, you didn't. I just … I'm not going to do this with you, Alex."

He looked genuinely confused. "Why?"

"Because of Stacy."

"Stacy?"

"I'm not going to do this with you when you're with her as well. I'm not going to share you with her."

"But—"

"No, Alex. Not when you're with her, too."

He looked at me for a long time, until I started to feel a little bit anxious. Finally, he spoke. "Stacy doesn't mean anything to me."

"Yet you go off with her almost every night to fool around with her."

"I'll stop. I'll tell her we have to stop."

Would he really do that? Did kissing and touching me mean that much to him? Or was he just looking for something new? Was he just getting bored with Stacy?

"It won't change things," I said.

"Why?"

"Because I'm not going to be a fling to you. I deserve more than that." It was hard to say that because I still wanted him, I still wanted to kiss him. I still wanted him to touch me. But my conviction was stronger, and I clung to it. "I'm not going to do stuff like that with you unless you want me the way I want you."

What am I saying? Did I just tell him I wanted to be with him? Is that what I was doing?

By the way he looked at me—with an intense focus and lingering desire—I could tell he was weighing my words, and coming to a conclusion.

"You want to be with me?" he asked, his gaze pinning me in place.

Geez! How could I answer that? I was too confused to say anything. Conflicting thoughts raced through my head. I wanted to shout out, "Yes! I'm so in love you!" But I also wanted to push him away again and yell at him, to tell him how much he'd been hurting me by running off with Stacy so often.

So I just stood there like an idiot and didn't say anything.

He kept his eyes on me, and I could see something click into place, an understanding settle in his eyes. "I understand," he said, his voice soft. After a few moments of silence, he spoke again.

"Let's eat. I'm starving."

And just like that—as if I hadn't just had the most amazing kiss of my life, as if I hadn't just confessed my feelings to Alex—I helped him get things ready.

As we ate, Alex's mood became almost cheerful, which I found odd, given what had just happened between us, and he casually asked me about my ninth-grade year. He started off with simple questions—which teachers and classes I'd liked best, what my schedule was like, what my daily life had been like—then became more and more personal.

"Were you with someone?" he asked.

"Ryan," I said.

"That kind of makes sense. Did he leave?"

"Yeah. He moved back to the States."

"Would you still be with him if he were still here?"

I shook my head as I scooped up the last of my chili. "No. I broke up with him a long time ago."

"Why?" Alex wiped his mouth with his napkin, then placed it in his empty bowl.

"Because I didn't love him."

He nodded in understanding. "I get it, you know."

"Get what?"

"I get why you would be with someone you don't love."

I had to be very, very careful with what I was about to ask. "Did … did you love Taylor?"

Alex leaned back in the seat, stretching his arms over his head. I waited to see how he would react to the mention of his dead girlfriend.

Surprisingly, he didn't seem bothered at all. He finished off his soda. "Nah. I liked her. She was fun. But I didn't love her. I thought I did, but that was before … " He trailed off.

Before what? What changed?

"Help me clean up?" he asked, rising to his feet. "Then I was thinking we could watch *Goonies* or something."

CHAPTER EIGHTEEN

I was running late that night because Mom sat me down and made me listen to her go on and on about the dangers of underage drinking, and how she was going to trust me to do the right thing if I found myself being pressured to drink. I did my best to put her at ease, reassuring her that I was a smart girl who would never do anything as reckless as drink alcohol, and the whole time I was thinking how I couldn't wait to get to the bleachers and get nice and buzzed.

If Mom only knew her little girl was turning bad.

So I left my house about thirty minutes later than usual. Halfway down my street, I saw Anna walking toward me. She was practically jogging.

When we met, she stood in front of me, her eyes wild.

"What did you do?" she asked breathlessly.

"What? What are you talking about?"

"Stacy's on the warpath. She's totally pissed at

you."

"Why would she be pissed at me? I didn't do anything to her." I began walking toward the commons and Anna fell in step beside me.

"Yeah, well, when I showed up at the bleachers Stacy was crying to Avery and telling her how she was going to kick your ass when she saw you. I had to tell her that if she wanted a go at you, she'd have to come through me first and that shut her up. She's been bitching about you for the past half-hour."

I took that in. "She's such a spaz. What's her deal? I haven't done anything to her. I haven't even seen her since—"

I stopped dead in my tracks.

Holy crap

He did it

He actually did it

"What?" Anna asked, standing in front of me. "Are you okay? You look like you just realized you're not wearing any panties."

"He broke up with her," I said.

"But they weren't together to begin with."

"Well, that's how she would take it. She thinks they're practically engaged."

Anna looked a little confused. "But why would he do that? I mean, unless he—" Her eyebrows shot up. "Holy crap."

"Yeah," I said.

"Holy crap," she said again. "He broke up with her

because he wants to be with you." Then her eyes got all accusatory. "What aren't you telling me? What happened?"

I quickly summarized my day with Alex. I told her about the kiss—glossing over how hot and mind-melting it had been—and how I'd basically confessed my feelings to him.

Anna's eyes were wide when I finished. "So you told him you wouldn't do sexy fun stuff with him if he was still with Stacy and then he goes off and breaks up with her? Holy crap, Chloe, he *so* wants to be with you. What are you going to do?"

I chewed on my lip, not sure how to answer. "I don't know," I said, then resumed walking.

"You have to do something. He's practically declaring his love for you."

"That's not true," I said. "Just because he broke up with Stacy doesn't mean he loves me. I'm not going to be one of his flings."

"Are you being serious? If he wanted a fling, he'd just stay with Stacy. He does *not* want a fling with you. You told him you wouldn't be with him if he was still with Stacy and then he goes and pretty much breaks up with her right away. How is that not declaring his love for you?"

I wasn't sure how to answer that.

"Please tell me you're not going to throw this opportunity away. This is Alex! You've only been in love with him for ten months. Haven't you been dreaming for this to happen? How are you not excited about this?"

"Because it's too good to be true," I whispered to myself.

When we approached the bleachers, I could see that Alex, Hudson, and London were already there. Alex was sitting off to the side on the top row like he usually did, but Stacy was on the far side of the bleachers, huddled together with Avery. Hudson and London were talking together, sharing a bottle.

I avoided Stacy and walked around the bleachers, then sat with Anna next to Hudson and London.

"Hey guys," I said, trying to ignore the death stare Stacy was giving me. I looked up to Alex. "Hi, Alex."

Is it true? Do you love me?

"Hey, Chloe." He looked peacefully content as he regarded me, his lips ever so slightly curled into a smile. Then he turned his attention back to the night and sipped from his bottle.

And that's how the evening played out. Anna, Hudson, London and I sat together, talking and sharing a bottle of sadiki, while Stacy and Avery sat to the side. I could feel Stacy's eyes on me all night long, but I did my best to ignore her. Alex, sitting behind me, stayed quiet, but when I would look over my shoulder at him, I saw that he was still staring off into the night, that same contented look on his face. Sometimes, he'd look down at me and give me a hint of a smile, and something in his eyes would reach out and caress me.

I hadn't had too much to drink, but I was still feeling really loose and warm. I'd sort of participated in the conversation less and less until I was just sitting there, thinking about Alex, what he'd done, and what it might mean.

So he broke up with Stacy or at least told her he wouldn't fool around with her anymore. And the only reason I could think of that he would do that was because I told him I wouldn't be with him if he was with Stacy, too. So it stood to reason that he wanted to be with me. I mean, he basically did what I told him he had to do to be with me. So why was he just sitting there, staring off into the distance, with that almost dopey look on his face? Why wasn't he telling me what he'd done? Why wasn't he asking me out? Why was he just sitting there?

And why was *I* just sitting there? Why couldn't I seem to think of anything to say to him?

Anna stood, grabbing my upper arm, dragging me up. "We're getting some fries," she told everyone, then pulled me along.

She waited until we were a good distance away. "What are you doing?" she asked, exasperated, as we made our way to the snack bar. "Why are you just sitting there like an idiot?"

"Well, he hasn't said anything to me. Why hasn't he said anything to me? It's kind of weird, right?" We stepped into the snack bar, and I moved to the side to let a woman and her kids by.

"It doesn't matter! *Everyone* knows he and Stacy aren't together now. It's so obvious. Did you not hear what London said to Hudson? She knows. He knows. Everyone knows! He's just waiting for you." She turned to the man behind the counter. "Large fries and two sodas, please."

After she paid, we went to sit at a table. The snack bar was mostly empty, with only one other table occupied.

"You're killing me, Chloe."

"I don't know what to say to him. I can't just say, 'so I heard you broke up with Stacy to be with me.'"

"Yes! You can! That's exactly what you should say."

"I'm not going to say that," I said, crossing my arms over my chest. "No way."

"Why not?"

"I ... I don't know. Because it's embarrassing."

"Argh! Why are you being such an idiot?"

"Would you settle down?"

"No. I will not settle down. Not until you agree to talk to him."

I let out a frustrated breath. "Okay! Okay. I'll talk to him. Just ... let me work up to it."

Anna beamed at me. "Have some food first. It'll clear your head."

So after eating our fries and downing our sodas wow, alcohol makes you thirsty , we walked back to the bleachers. Everyone was seated right where we had left them.

As we drew near, Alex was watching me, that same frustrating half-smile on his face. I hesitated, but Anna not so subtly pushed me forward. "Talk. To. Him."

Right Here we go

I climbed the bleachers as Alex continued to watch me. When I reached him, I stood there for a moment, gathering up my nerve. "Can we talk?"

He nodded, then stood. "Sure. Let's go to the playground."

I was surprised when he grabbed my hand and led me down the steps to the ground. He didn't let go as we walked to the playground. We sat side by side on a bench, so close our legs were touching.

Alex was still holding my hand.

I glanced at his face to find him looking back at me with tenderness in his eyes. "You broke up with Stacy," I said in a quieter voice than I had intended.

"I wasn't going out with her."

"You know what I mean."

"I do. And, yes, I broke up with her."

"Why?"

"Because you wanted me to."

I studied his face, looking for the hidden meaning I was looking for. "Alex ... that's not enough for me. I don't want to be just a fling to you. I'm not going to kiss you and stuff if you just want to get in my pants."

He squeezed my hand and gave me that lazy half-smile. "That's not what this is about, Chloe."

"Then what is it about?"

"It's about you."

"Me?"

"Yes." He rubbed his thumb across my hand, gently and delicately, sending shivers up my spine. "I want you to know that you matter to me. That you're important to me. I want you to know that you've made a difference in my life. You're what keeps me going, Chloe. When I go to bed at night, I'm thinking of you. How you'll come wake me up in the morning. How I'll be able to get out of bed because you'll be there. And if I'm having ... if I'm having a rough time, I know you'll stay with me. I know you'll be there for me." He paused, looking ahead of him. "You're my one thing, Chloe. There's only you."

I was stunned. I wasn't sure what I'd expected him to say, but it certainly wasn't that. I never expected him to open up to me that way, and I totally hadn't anticipated his words, or feeling their meaning so deeply.

I felt my eyes well up, and I had to take a moment to compose myself, to wrap my head around what Alex had just said. I had no idea he felt that way about me. I thought I was just a girl he liked to hang out with. Yes, he'd opened up to me twice—when he wasn't doing well—but I thought that was simply because I was there. I was just a girl he'd known for a few weeks.

But ...

His words made me feel like I was special, like I was giving him something he couldn't get from anyone else.

Alex needed me.

"You're important to me, too," I finally said. "I want you to know that I'm not going to run away. I'll be here for you. When you're feeling sad, I'll be with you."

"I know." He reached out to me, caressed my cheek and leaned over, delicately pressing his lips on mine. It was tender and soft, but not tentative. He kissed me like it was the most natural thing in the world to him, like he'd been doing it for years.

I kissed him back, feeling the warmth of his lips and the nearness of him, and it made me realize that this, what I was doing right now, was what I wanted from him. For the first time since I'd met him, I felt like I was his and he was mine.

We pulled away from each other, our eyes locked.

"That was nice," I said.

"Yeah, it was."

We went back to the bleachers, hand in hand, and we sat close together, slightly apart from the others. Anna, Hudson, and London didn't say anything, but they each caught my eyes, nodded, and smiled approvingly. London's expression was almost grateful. Stacy, however, didn't react so well. She stood, her eyes full of tears, and gave me a hurt look, like I'd betrayed her. Then she ran off. Avery, after a few moments, followed her.

I refused to feel bad. Alex had made his choice, and he chose me. She would just have to deal with it.

Later, when I had to go home, Alex kissed me goodnight, and I walked home feeling happier than I ever thought I'd be.

It was only after I'd crawled into bed and turned off the light that it occurred to me that Alex had never asked me out. He'd never actually asked me to be his girlfriend. Was I just assuming we were together now?

No.

His words had said enough. He told me I was his one thing. What else could it mean?

CHAPTER NINETEEN

I woke up feeling excited and wanting to see Alex as soon as I could. I cleaned up my room, ate breakfast, and helped Mom with the dishes.

"I spoke with Alex's father," Mom said, stopping me just as I was about to leave. "He said he's known that Alex has been struggling, but the poor man had no idea that Alex has been behaving so recklessly. He agreed to speak with Alex. How has he been?"

"Better," I said. "He stayed in his house for two days, but when he finally came out, he seemed to be doing much better. He laughs and smiles now. It's like he's trying his best to deal with what happened. I think he's going to be okay."

"That's good to hear. But ... "

Uh-oh

"I'm not comfortable with you being around him and his friends when they're drinking."

I took in a breath and tried to be as cool as possible

because I didn't want to antagonize her. "But, Mom, they all hang out together. If I can't hang out with Alex, then I can't hang out with any of them. You might as well ground me for the rest of the summer. Please don't tell me not to see them."

She sighed, a reluctant acceptance on her face. "I know, honey. I know. With so few of you here, you don't really have anyone else to spend time with, and I don't want to isolate you from your friends. But I worry. You are all too young to be drinking. It scares me."

"We just hang out, Mom," I said, trying not sound whiny. "We just sit at the bleachers or the playground talking. They're not doing anything bad."

"You know it makes me a bad mother to let this continue, right? I should be calling their parents and letting them know what their kids are doing. That's what a responsible parent would do."

Oh my god, that would be a disaster! "But then everyone would get in trouble, and we'd all be grounded, and I'd spend my entire summer alone. Please, Mom. Please don't call their parents. Please. It would ruin the whole summer."

Mom nodded, then sighed heavily. "I know, and I don't want that to happen. So I'm going to keep quiet, and I won't tell your father. But you have to promise me you won't drink, and that you'll tell me if things start to get out of hand. I'm trusting you, Chloe. Please don't let me down."

I was starting to feel pretty bad about myself. I'd already lied about my not drinking, and I'd done it even after promising I wouldn't. But now things were different. Mom was willing to take a risk for me. I knew I couldn't break her trust.

"I promise," I said, meaning it. "I won't drink."

"I believe you, Chloe. I know you'll make good choices. Now, go on. Go have fun with your friends. That's what summer is for."

She ushered me out the door, sending me on my way.

The front door at Alex's house was unlocked, so I let myself in. Alex was asleep on his bed, tangled up in his sheets, as usual, looking good enough to eat. I watched him as he slept, taking in his bare back, his sexy shoulders, his tussled hair. His face was peaceful, and he looked like he didn't have a care in the world.

As I moved toward the window to open the blinds, I bumped his desk chair, and it knocked over a notebook that had been lying precariously on his desk.

Alex didn't stir.

I reached down and grabbed the notebook, intent on putting it back on the desk, but the writing on it caught my attention. A poem was written in the middle of the page.

I knew I shouldn't, that I was invading his privacy, but I wanted to know what he'd written. I wanted to know what he thought about when he was alone.

I turned so my back was to Alex, and I read the poem.

She says fly free
let it go, come with me
She doesn't know
She'll never see
the stars have disappeared for me

She cries for me
but I can't forgive
She doesn't know
She'll never see
this broken life I can't relive

She waits for me
my soul forsaken
She doesn't know
She'll never see
there is no light to awaken

She doesn't know

I reread the poem. Twice. Three times. But the message didn't change. This was Alex's pain.

A tear slid down my cheek and I wiped it away, then quickly closed the notebook and placed it back on the desk.

Is that how Alex was feeling? Did he really feel that

hopeless? Did he feel he was beyond saving?

And was I the girl in the poem?

I turned around and nearly gasped. Alex was awake, on his side, watching me.

Oh no

Had he seen?

"Hey, Chloe," he said lazily, then grinned at me.

Okay. That was good. He wasn't angry. He might not have seen me reading his poem. "Hi, Alex. Time to get up."

He watched me, still grinning. "You need to leave. I'm naked."

"Oh!" I blushed, then hurried to the door. "Right. I'll wait for you."

Twenty minutes later, after I'd finished Alex's chores, he stepped into the kitchen wearing swim trunks and a tank top. He rubbed at his head, messing up his hair.

In his other hand, he held a LEGO submarine.

"So we're going to the pool?" I asked.

"Yeah. I have to call Hudson though, so he'll bring his sub."

After a quick call, we headed out. As we walked, Alex held my hand. His stride was quick like he couldn't wait to get to the pool, and I had to rush to keep up with him. But he never let go of my hand.

Only London was there, laying out in her tiny bikini on her lounge chair, looking like a goddess. When we reached her, she sat up, watching us.

A spectacular smile formed on her face. "Hey, guys!"

I laid out my towel on the chair next to her and sat. Alex sat on the ground and began dismantling his submarine. He looked content, so I just left him alone, glad that he was enjoying himself.

Not long after, Hudson showed up with his LEGO ship. He sat with Alex, and the two of them began to make boasts and disparaging remarks to each other as they rebuilt their ships.

A few minutes later, Anna and Avery arrived. Stacy wasn't with them, and I wondered if she would show up at all.

The morning passed lazily and without concern. Alex's good mood seemed to surprise everyone. He wasn't quite where I'd seen him last summer—I knew his pain was just under the surface—but he appeared to be doing his best. He was trying.

After lunch, and after we'd laid out for a while, we all got in the pool to cool off. Alex and Hudson had already had several submarine challenges, so now they spent time with the girls. Alex was always by me, touching me sometimes when we talked, and when I looked his direction, his eyes were usually on me. He would give me a grin, or even a wink, then move in close to me.

When we got out of the pool and laid out again, I noticed that London and Avery were still in the water, standing close and talking. Then they pulled themselves out of the pool and walked toward the girls' locker room.

Avery's expression was blank like it usually was, but poor London looked so nervous I thought she might start crying. They both disappeared into the locker room and stayed in there for a long time.

Eventually, they both came out and walked over to us, London in the lead. She looked like she couldn't contain herself, and Avery, who kept touching her lips, had an almost amazed look on her face.

Avery immediately began to gather her stuff.

"Leaving already?" Anna asked her.

"I have to go shopping in town with my parents."

"Oh," I said. "Will you be out later?"

"Yes. I'll see you guys later."

As Avery walked away, London leaned in close. "Can we talk?" she asked in an excited whisper. "Alone?"

"Sure."

She latched onto my wrist and led me into the shade under the pavilion. She took me to the far end, and we sat at a picnic table.

London looked so happy I thought she might burst.

"She said she wants to try," she said to me excitedly.

"Avery?"

"Yes! She told me she couldn't stop thinking of me."

"London, that's great!"

"We kissed," London went on. "A lot."

A little laugh escaped me, realizing why Avery had looked so befuddled. "I'm so happy for you, London. I'm really glad it's working out for you."

"Me too. And since we're going to the same boarding school we can be together there too. I can't believe it!"

"That's awesome, London."

"Thanks." She leaned in closer. "I wanted to tell you something else, too."

"Okay."

"I'm really glad you and Alex are together now. I've been so worried about him because of what happened to his girlfriend, but I know you've been there for him. I love him, but I know I can't give him what he needs right now. He needs you. You're really good for him. He's better when he's with you."

I guess I shouldn't have been surprised that she'd been watching him so closely. And I was glad to have her approval; that meant a lot to me.

It didn't escape my notice that she was assuming Alex and I were together. That was good to hear. I knew I'd have to talk to Alex about that later, to see if we were both on the same page, but for now, I was content just to be with him

"Thanks, London."

Then we shared a grin and laughed, knowing that we had just become closer.

The rest of the day passed by quietly. We were together, enjoying each other's company on a lazy summer day, and I was beginning to think that everything would be okay.

But I couldn't get Alex's poem out of my thoughts. I knew he was still hurting. He was still in pain. And I knew that he still needed me.

He was trying, though. His sudden mood change after the light tower incident proved that. But I knew he needed help. He needed support. He needed me.

I swore to myself then that I would do whatever it took to help Alex, to help him deal with his anguish. I was willing to give him everything I had.

We were so bored that night that instead of hanging out the bleachers, we decided to watch movies at Anna's house because her parents were out. So after dinner, we got together at her place for an *Alien* and *Aliens* marathon. I'd never seen either movie, and I was a little nervous about *Alien* because Anna kept going on about how scary it was. I didn't deal so well with scary movies.

I sat on the sofa with Alex, and London on the other side of him. Alex and I sat right up against each other, so our bodies were touching, and as the movie started, he held my hand on my thigh.

When the movie started getting scary, I snuggled up as close to him as I could, and he put his arm around me, whispering in my ear that I was a wimp.

"I can't help it," I said, then elbowed him in the ribs. "I hate scary movies."

He didn't say anything to that, but soon after he moved his arm and placed his palm down fully on my bare thigh. My breath hitched as he began to rub his fingers against my skin, and I started to lose focus on the movie. He kept up his lazy caress, stroking his fingers sensually over my skin, making a nice, soft warmth tighten low in my belly.

He touched me that way for the rest of the movie, and it wasn't until it was over that I realized I'd been so focused on the way Alex was touching me, that I never once got scared during the movie.

We had a break to use the bathroom and have snacks, then started *Aliens*, which, I was glad to find out, was more of an action flick than a horror.

Alex and I sat at our same spot, and once the movie started, he put his arm around me. I snuggled into him, wondering if he was going to touch me the same way again.

It wasn't long before I had my answer. He began to softly run his fingers along my upper arm, sending the most amazing pulses through my body. Sometimes his fingers would brush my breast, which was alarming at first, but then began to make me aroused. I just sat there, focused on his touches, as I got more and more turned on.

I could hardly believe how crazy he was making me

feel.

I had a hard time concentrating on *Aliens*, too.

The movie ended shortly before I had to go home. I said goodnight to everyone and stepped out onto the front porch. Alex followed me.

"I'll walk you home," he said, taking my hand.

We headed out together, walking side by side.

"So what did you think of the movies?" he asked.

"Well, I was a little bit distracted, so I can't really say."

"Oh yeah? You were distracted?"

"I think you know I was."

He chuckled. "Mission accomplished."

I smacked his arm, teasing. "I'll get you back for that."

"I look forward to it," he said.

Soon we were standing on my front patio.

"Hey," he said, leaning close. "Come to my house tonight."

My eyebrows shot up. Was he suggesting ... "You mean sneak out?"

"Yeah."

"Are you crazy? Do you have any idea how much trouble I'll be in if my parents catch me?"

He shrugged. "So don't get caught. It's easy. I do it all the time. When do your parents go to bed?"

"Around midnight, I think."

"Okay, so after they go to bed, wait about an hour, then sneak out your window."

Oh my god, I couldn't believe I was even considering this. Then I remembered my promise to Mom. "Are you going to drink?"

"No."

Okay, that was good. "So you want me to sneak out and come to your house?"

"Yeah. I'll wait for you."

"Then what?"

"I want to take you somewhere. I want to talk to you. I have something to tell you."

I wasn't sure what that could be, but I could tell by the sudden change in his tone that he considered this important, that he didn't want to go out just for the sake of it. I realized that he was asking me to be with him, that he needed me.

I couldn't say no to that.

"Okay. I'll come over around one in the morning. Will you be up?"

He nodded. "Yeah. I'll be up. Just knock on my window."

"Okay." I stood on my toes and gave him a quick kiss on his lips. "I'll be there."

CHAPTER TWENTY

Alex was right. Sneaking out was easy. I was in bed, reading, when my parents came in to say goodnight. I told them I was going to bed too, and turned off my light as they left. Then I waited.

It was as simple as opening my window, removing the screen, and quietly slipping out into the night. I moved silently through the dark shadows between the houses. When I had to cross a lighted street, I made sure there was no one in view, then dashed across.

It only took about ten minutes to get to Alex's house. All the lights were off in the front, so I made my way to the back of the house where I found Alex's bedroom light on. I tapped on his window, hoping that his dad wasn't in the room with him. I dashed off to the side of the house, and peeked around the corner, just in case.

Alex appeared in the window, looking around. I stepped out of the shadows and approached. Since he was leaning out of the window, his head was level with mine, so I leaned into him and kissed him.

"Hey, you," I said. "Here I am."

"Hold on," he said, and with just those two words I knew his mood was serious.

He went back into his room, turned off the light, then crawled out of his window.

"Where are we going?" I asked.

"316."

That made me a little bit uneasy. "Alex, you said you wouldn't drink."

"I won't," he replied as he grabbed my hand and led me along. "It's just nice there. No one will bother us."

Sneaking to 316 took considerably longer because it was in another camp, but by sticking to the shadows and running like hell across the open spaces, we eventually made it.

The back patio door was unlocked, just like Alex said it would be. It was quiet inside, and fairly well-lit from the street lights outside. The furniture was arranged like someone still lived in the house.

Alex led me to the sofa, and we sat next to each other. I wasn't exactly sure what Alex had planned, so I sat quietly. Were we going to make out? Do more? Was I ready for that?

I waited.

But Alex didn't say or do anything. He just sat there, his gaze cast down to his hand on my leg. Even in the dark, I could see his expression change. It was like watching a sudden storm come in, dark and full of turmoil.

I instinctively knew something was wrong.

"Alex?"

He didn't look at me.

"Alex. Why are we here? Please look at me."

But he wouldn't. "I'm ... thinking," he said, his voice full of emotion.

"About what?"

"I ... I need to tell you something. But I ... it's hard."

I placed my hand over his. "It's okay. Take your time. I'll wait."

Alex stayed quiet for a long time. Then tears streamed from his eyes, and he squeezed my hand tightly. "It's about Taylor," he finally said, his voice low and heavy with pain.

I twisted to the side, so I was facing him. I took his hand in both of mine. "There was nothing you could have done, Alex. She was going to die whether you went for help or not. At least she didn't die alone."

"You don't understand," he said, his voice breaking. "You don't understand."

"I understand that it was an accident. That you couldn't do anything about it. I understand that you stayed with her so she wouldn't be alone. I know that you—"

"I killed her," he blurted out, taking his hands

from mine and hugging himself. He began to rock back and forth. "I killed her."

"Alex, no ... you didn't. It was an accident."

"She died because of me." His voice was trembling now, and he looked like he was barely hanging on. "I killed her."

"That's not true. Please don't—"

"When she was on the cliff ... when she was scared ... I started to climb back down to help her. But ..." Alex's face crumpled then, and a low moan tore out of him. "Oh god. Oh god. Oh god." He rocked back and forth, his face tortured.

I leaned into him, bringing him down to me so I could hold him tight. He collapsed into me. "It's okay, Alex. It's okay."

"I slipped," he said quietly. "I slipped, and I knocked her off the cliff. She fell because I hit her. She died because of me. I killed her."

I was beginning to understand. Alex hadn't been struggling with grief all summer. He'd been consumed with guilt. It was beginning to make sense. "No, you didn't kill her. It was an accident."

"I didn't mean to do it," he said, his breath catching. "I didn't mean to kill her. Please believe me."

"I believe you. Have you not told anyone else about this?"

"No. Just you. No one else knows."

I was touched. Alex trusted me enough to share his deepest, darkest secret, something he hadn't shared

231

with anyone else. And I knew he needed me to make things better for him.

Alex cried silently, leaning against me, for a long time. I simply sat next to him, holding him, and trailing my fingers over his arm. Now and then I whispered to him, telling him that it was going to be okay, that I was there for him.

He sat up suddenly, looking up at the ceiling. "I hurt, Chloe. I hurt so bad. I want it to stop. I just want it to stop. Please make it stop."

My heart clenched painfully tight. His voice was so full of pain and anguish that it nearly overwhelmed me, and I got scared. What could I possibly do to make this better for him? What could I do to make him forget, even if just for a little while?

I lifted myself up, hitched my skirt up, and swung my leg around, so I was straddling him. I pushed him back against the cushion.

"Chloe ... what are—"

"Shhh."

Then with the full power of the pain we were sharing, I kissed him desperately. I forced my tongue into his mouth and he jolted with surprise. I pressed up against him and my body reacted, the intensity of my arousal surprising me. It was like I'd walked off a ledge and was falling, falling, falling into something I wasn't sure I could get out of.

Alex returned my kiss with a fierceness that only drew me in further. We kissed frantically like we might die if we stopped, and our hands roamed over each other's bodies, needing more and more and more, but not quite grasping what we desired. I was so aroused I thought I might scream.

His hands slipped up my back, under my shirt, and with surprising ease, he unclasped my bra.

I became nervous then, alarmed at finding myself almost lost in my burning desire, and I wondered how much further I was willing to let this go.

But his hands ... his lips ... his moans ... they were calling me back, seducing me, making it almost impossible for me to hold onto rational thought. I was so conflicted, and I struggled with indecision, not knowing what to do. I'd started this, hoping to give him something other than his guilt to focus on, wanting to make his pain go away, however briefly. But I hadn't thought it through, hadn't anticipated the passion that was raging between us.

Alex crushed me to him as his hands roamed over my bare back. "I love you," he whispered in my ear. "I love you so much."

"You love me?" I asked between gasps, between kisses.

"I've always loved you. It's only ever been just you."

I made my choice. I spoke, my voice low. "Take me to a bedroom."

When I awoke, I knew three things.

One, it was 5:23 in the morning, and the early light of predawn was beginning to brighten the room.

Two, I wasn't at home.

And three, I'd just had unprotected sex.

I knew I should have been most concerned about the last, but it was the first two that made me sit up in a panic.

"Crap! Alex! Get up!"

He must have sensed my panic, because he shot up out of bed, as naked as I was.

"Oh my god, oh my god, oh my god," I said in a rush. "I am going to be in so much trouble. Alex! Get dressed! We have to get home!"

I'd never dressed so quickly in my life. We were outside in minutes. The sun hadn't risen yet, but the eastern sky was glowing pink and purple.

I whirled toward Alex, reached up and grabbed his face with both of my hands. I kissed him hard and fast. "If I'm not grounded forever, I'll come wake you up. I love you."

"I love you, too."

And with that I raced home, hoping with all my might that my parents hadn't discovered that I wasn't at home.

"You look tired, Chloe. Did you not sleep well?"

I almost laughed at that. If Mom only knew why I was tired. I stopped at the door, holding it open as I looked over my shoulder. "Not really. I kept waking up. But I'm okay. Breakfast helped. I'm off to the pool."

"Bye, honey. Have fun."

I stepped out, closed the door, and all but ran to Alex's house. I had to talk to him. We had to figure out what we were going to do if I became pregnant. I had this terrifying feeling, a near certainty, that that's exactly what was going to happen. I wasn't experienced with this sort of thing, but I wasn't stupid. My last period was two weeks ago. I knew this was the worst possible time to have unprotected sex.

And how the hell would I tell my parents? How was I going to tell them that their fourteen-year-old daughter was pregnant?

By the time I got to Alex's house, I was so nervous and freaked out I was practically shaking.

The door was unlocked, so I stepped in, walking through the living room in a hurry to get to Alex's room and wake him up.

"Alex! I—"

I stopped at the kitchen entrance, my heart frozen, ice in my veins, as I took in what was before me.

Alex was on the kitchen floor, propped up against the cabinet, his leg splayed out in front of him.

His eyes were closed.

And there was blood.

So much blood.

I blinked stupidly, then noticed that a kitchen knife was pushed through his wrist, and that blood was seeping out of the wound.

I didn't scream. I didn't make a sound because I couldn't. I couldn't even breathe. I just stood there uselessly, staring at Alex laying on the floor, his head lolled to the side.

He looked so pale.

"Alex!" Hearing his name tear out of me was so surprising that it shook me out of my stunned inaction.

Stop the bleeding I have to stop the bleeding

I looked around, just barely holding off my panic. An apron. There was an apron. Apron strings. A tourniquet. I could make a tourniquet.

I tore open the drawer, grabbed the scissors. The apron was in my hands. I was cutting.

Then I was kneeling in the blood next to Alex, lifting his arm. I was wrapping, tying off the string as tight as I could, hoping it would be enough.

Mom Call Mom She'll know what to do

I was at the phone in seconds, struggling to pick up the handset because my hands were covered in slick blood. It seemed like hours before I managed to dial my number.

It rang.

And rang.

And I could only think that Alex was dying.

"Answer the phone!" I screamed and was rewarded two rings later.

"Parker residence."

"Mom! Mom! It's Alex!" I had to stop because a wave of nausea crashed over me.

"Chloe? What's wrong? Chloe? Where are you? What's going on?"

I forced the words out, swallowing bile. "It's Alex! He slit his wrist! There's so much blood, Mom! There's so much blood! I didn't know what to do! I made a tourniquet. Mom, please do something! Please, you have to do something!"

"Chloe, where are you?"

"At Alex's house."

"How long has he been bleeding?"

"I don't know. A while, I think. Please, Mom. He's going to die. Please do something."

"I'm going to hang up and call emergency services. They'll be there as soon as possible. But in the meantime, you need to stop the bleeding. Find whatever you can to make more tourniquets and tie them around his bicep and elbow. Make sure his arm is elevated. Don't leave him. I'll be there as soon as I can."

She hung up, and I ran back to the kitchen, grabbing the scissors and the apron. As fast as I could I cut out several strips, then kneeled by him. I struggled with his arm, doing my best to wrap the strips of cloth around it, then tying them off as tight as I could.

I tried to stand, but my knees slipped in the blood, and I almost fell over. So I stayed on my knees and with shaking arms lowered Alex prone on the ground. I sat next to him, holding his arm straight up, just like Mom had said, and waited for help to arrive.

It took several seconds for me to realize that the desperate cries that I was hearing were coming from my body.

Please don't die Please

I stayed at home that day, hiding in my room, and I cried and cried and cried, sobbing like my world had ended. Mom tried to comfort me, but I pushed her away, just wanting to be alone, hoping beyond hope that Alex hadn't died. That he would live.

The girls and Hudson came to see me that evening, wanting to know where Alex and I had been, but I couldn't talk to them. The words just wouldn't come. Mom had to step in, and in whispered tones, she told them what had happened. I heard London's sorrowful wail, then after a few minutes, there was silence again.

I didn't leave my room.

It had been dark for a couple of hours when my mom came into the room and sat beside me on the bed where I'd been curled up.

"He's going to be okay," she said, her voice

soothing. "His father just called."

I sat up, my limbs feeling weak. "He's alive?"

"Yes, honey. He needed a lot of blood, but he's okay now."

The relief I felt was so intense I could only let go. All the emotion I'd been struggling with since finding Alex at his house poured out of me in a flood, and I threw myself at my mother, clinging to her as I wept.

She caught me and held me tight as I cried.

We didn't hear anything for two days. I stayed inside my house, spending the day drawing and reading Alex's stories. Hudson and the girls visited the first night, and we gathered in my room. We were silent, no one knowing what to say, and we paired off. Anna sat with me on my bed, holding my hand. Hudson held London, who looked like she'd died inside. Avery and Stacy stood close to each other, Stacy's face wet with tears. Then they left, leaving me alone with my pain.

On the third day, my dad told us that Alex and his father had left the country.

Four weeks later I found out I was pregnant.

CHAPTER TWENTY-ONE

I carefully put Tyler in his crib, wondering if he'd fall asleep. It was nap time, but sometimes it was hard to tell if he was ready because he was such a calm baby. He tended to play quietly, only laughing when something really caught his interest, and making a fuss only when he was particularly grumpy. Today, he had played quietly in his playpen, allowing me to clean up the living room. I was so happy he wasn't a hyper baby— I'd been lucky. I cooed at him, watching as he sat and gripped a toy in his tiny hand. My heart swelled with love and pride, and I was thankful, like always, that I had him in my life, that I'd fought hard to keep him. He was everything to me.

The past two years hadn't been easy. At the end of that summer, Mom and I moved back to the US, in

North Carolina. Dad was staying another year in Saudi and would then come home and start his next assignment at Seymour Johnson Air Force Base. So it was just me and Mom. By that time I was almost two months pregnant.

We settled into our new home, and I started my sophomore year. I waited an entire month more before telling my mom. She was shocked at first, and had cried, but she didn't freak out. I had been afraid that she would demand I get an abortion, but it never came up. Instead, Mom urged me to put the baby up for adoption. She was relentless, saying that a baby would be too much for me to handle and that she didn't want my life to be hard. She left adoption agency pamphlets all over the house and mentioned adoption every chance she got. I fought with her almost daily. Then one day she made an appointment with a social worker and told me I had to go along with it. That night I packed a bag, stole some money from Mom's wallet, and ran away to Aunt Kelly in Maryland. It took two weeks, but my parents came to accept my determination to keep my baby, and I came home.

From then on, Mom and Dad were supportive. They let me know that they would help me raise my baby, that I wouldn't have to go through it alone, and that they would support me while I went to school. As my due date approached, Mom became more and more excited, and she went a little bit nuts buying clothes and toys and all the other things I would need when the baby came.

I was so relieved.

But after Tyler was born, things weren't easy even with my parents' help. My life revolved around my son and school. Between taking care of Tyler and studying, I didn't have time for friends or any kind of social life. But I was fine with that. I was a mother, and I was fully committed to my son. He was what I lived for.

I watched Tyler as he played, and as happened so often, I was reminded of Alex—Tyler had his father's eyes. Remembering Alex meant stirring up the pain and the anger over what he had done to me. I gave myself to him, and he still went through with his plans to kill himself. He told me he loved me, but he knew I would find his body. Even now, despite two years of therapy, I was still haunted by the way I had found Alex that morning. I still had nightmares about it.

In fact, the night I spent with him was the last peaceful night I'd had in two years.

Then, at the age of fifteen, I gave birth to Tyler.

But the memories weren't all bad. Sometimes I remembered him as the bright, happy boy I'd fallen in love with, and how we'd become so close that summer. I remembered our love, and that made me smile, because despite everything, I was still in love with him.

I didn't think that would ever change.

And I wished—sometimes so much that it hurt— that Alex was in my life, that he was here with Tyler and me. I wished we were a family. But I knew that was hopeless. I had no idea where Alex was, and in two years, he hadn't tried to contact me.

I made sure the monitor was on before I left Tyler. I went to the living room and made sure everything was picked up.

I was alone in the house. Dad was at work, and Mom had gone out shopping, wanting to give me privacy.

I was having a guest.

Anna was coming over.

She was the only one of my friends from Taif that I'd managed to keep in contact with. Over the past two years, we'd written each other almost every week and talked on the phone every few months. She was still the closest friend I had.

Anna had turned seventeen two months ago and had convinced her parents that she was old enough to drive on her own from Georgia to see me. We'd been planning it for months.

She would be here any moment.

I never heard a car pull up in the driveway, so I was surprised when the doorbell rang.

My heart pounded in excitement.

I rushed to the door and threw it open.

Anna was there, smiling her brilliant smile. Tears filled my eyes as we threw ourselves at each other and embraced in a tight hug. I buried my face in her neck, trying to keep my composure.

"It's so good to see you, Anna," I said, my voice

full of emotion. After a few silent moments, I pulled away to look at her. Her cheeks were wet with tears, but she was smiling, her eyes bright, looking happy.

"It's so good to see you, too, girl," she said. "I've missed you so much."

I grabbed her hand and pulled her into the house. "Come in. Come sit."

We sat together on the sofa and studied each other, both of us with goofy grins on our faces.

"I can't believe you're here," I said.

"Yep. I'm here. Alive and kicking."

"When did you cut your hair?"

"Two weeks ago," she said, running her hands through her short hair. "Do you like it?"

"Yeah. I do. You look great. But why didn't you say anything?" We'd talked on the phone twice in the past two weeks, and she'd never mentioned her hair.

"I wanted to surprise you. Are your parents here?"

I shook my head. "No. Dad's at work and Mom left for a few hours. We're alone. How was the drive?"

"No problem. It was good."

"Were your parents still okay with you coming?"

Anna snorted a laugh. "My mom was trying to be cool about it, but she was just short of freaking out. She hovered all morning. You'd think I was driving across the country by the way she was acting. Dad had to keep assuring her that I would be okay. I need to call them, though, to let them know I got here okay. Can I use your phone?"

"Sure. It's right over there."

"Thanks."

I waited as Anna talked to her mom.

"Yes, Mom, I'm fine," Anna said patiently. "Yes, I'm sure. I know, Mom. Would you relax? The drive was fine. Yes, really. Mom! I said I'm fine. Chloe is waiting for me—I need to go. Yes, I'll call you tomorrow. Promise. Okay. I love you, too. Bye."

Anna hung up, looked at me and rolled her eyes. "Sheesh ... she can be such a pain."

I laughed. "I know what you mean. My mom worried all through my pregnancy. She was more nervous than I was." I clapped my palms on my thighs and stood up. "Speaking of, do you want to see Tyler?"

Anna stood to face me, but her eyes avoided mine. "Wait," she said, and I was surprised by the sudden nervousness in her voice.

"What is it?"

"I ... um ... I brought ... " she paused. "There's something you need to see."

"Oh?"

"Yeah. It's ... it's going to be a big shock, so I want you to be prepared."

That made me anxious and a little scared. "Did something happen, Anna? Are you okay?"

"No! Nothing happened. Well, I mean, sort of. But I'm okay. It's nothing bad. At least I hope it's not. Promise me you won't freak out."

"You're kind of freaking me out already. Just tell

me."

She stepped away, toward the door. "I'm just going to my car. I'll be right back."

I nodded. "Okay."

I watched her leave through the thin, gauzy curtains of the living room window. She walked down the driveway and to a white sedan parked in front of the neighbor's house. *hy did she park way over there?* She went to the passenger side of the car and opened the door. I couldn't quite make out what she was doing, but it looked like she was talking to someone.

Then a person stepped out of the car, a young guy.

ho is that?

The two of them made their way back to the house. I watched as they approached, and as they got closer, I began to make out the details of the boy's face.

Oh my god

I gasped, my hand over my mouth, and stepped back, nearly tumbling over the coffee table.

I ran to the door and opened it.

It was Alex.

Suddenly it felt like all the air in the world had disappeared. I struggled to make sense of what I was seeing, wondering if I was dreaming. It couldn't be. It just couldn't be. That couldn't possibly be Alex.

But it was.

I stared, taking him in. He was dressed in jeans and a black T-shirt, and his hair was longer than I remembered. It almost reached his shoulders.

Conflicting emotions exploded within me, swirling around violently like a tempest, keeping me from feeling any one thing. But then one single, powerful emotion that I'd been struggling with for so long rose up within me.

I walked purposefully toward them, every muscle in my body clenched.

When I reached them, I stood in front of Alex for a few seconds. Then my hand shot out, and I slapped him across the face, as hard as I could, making his head snap to the side.

But I wasn't finished. I stepped up close and shoved him away, hard. "How could you!" The words tore out of me, angry and hard, and I pushed him away again.

"Chloe," Anna said, grabbing me. "Calm down."

I shook her off, still facing Alex, who looked back at me, his face sorrowful.

"How could you!" I shouted at him again, my voice wavering. "How could you do that to me!"

"I—" he began, but I cut him off.

"You knew I would find you! You knew I was coming to get you! You knew I was going to find your body! And you did it anyway! Do you know what that was like for me? Do you know what I went through? You, of all people, should have known better!"

I waited for him to say something, anything, but he just looked back at me, his eyes full of regret and acceptance. But there was a determination there, too. He stood without flinching as my angry words had crashed over him. He wasn't going to back down. He wasn't going to run away.

I slumped, my shoulders dropping. The anger was gone. It had ripped out of me, releasing two years of pent-up emotion in a sudden, violent rush, and now I was left feeling empty and hurt. "Why did you leave me, Alex?" I asked in a whisper, my head hanging low. "Why did you leave me all alone?"

He stepped forward and reached toward me, his hand hovering just inches from my face. Then he cupped my chin and brought my head up so I would look at him. "I don't have the answers you need, Chloe. I don't have reasons or excuses. I can only ask for your forgiveness. I can only say that I'm sorry for what I did. I'm sorry you had to find me that way. And I'm sorry that I left you alone. I'm so sorry."

He started to pull his hand away, but I grabbed it and held it against my cheek, remembering how he had touched me before, and how good it made me feel.

I wanted to feel that way again. Buried under two years of anger, I still longed for his touch.

Anna touched my shoulder. "We should take this inside. Your neighbors are watching."

"Come with me," I said to Alex and grabbed his hand. "We need to talk."

I led Alex into the house. "Have a seat." I gestured to the sofa.

Anna, who had followed us, touched my shoulder again. "I'll go see Tyler," she whispered. "Give you some privacy. I'll find my way."

"Thanks." As Anna walked away, I sat on the sofa, my body angled toward Alex so we could look at each other. Alex's face was bright red where I'd slapped him.

"I'm sorry I hit you," I said quietly.

"I deserved it."

"Yes. You did." I paused, trying to gather my thoughts. "Why did you come here, Alex?"

"I ... I came to apologize. And to thank you for saving my life." His eyes held me, and I could see the sincerity on his face. He was calm, with confident determination. "I've been looking for you for a year."

"You have?" Had he been thinking of me that long? "How did you find me?"

Alex twisted so he could face me. "When I left Saudi, I was in a really bad place, and I had to focus on getting better. I never forgot you, Chloe, but I wasn't well enough to try to find you. It took me almost a year to get better. But you were in my thoughts all the time, and I realized that I needed to find you, no matter what it took."

I didn't know what to make of that. To hear him say that he'd been thinking of me all this time, just like I'd been thinking of him, made my resentment ebb slightly, and I was touched. But I also felt concerned. It took him a year to get better? Had he been in a hospital? I knew from my talks with Sarah, my therapist, that people who attempted suicide were often admitted to mental hospitals and kept there, sometimes for weeks or months, until they got better. Is that what had happened to him?

"I had no idea where you were, though," Alex went on. "I lost contact with everyone. My only hope was Hudson, but by the time I wrote him, he'd already left school and moved back to the States. I didn't know where he'd gone. I tried London and Avery, but they'd left their school, too. I didn't know what else to do so I asked my dad for help, and he wrote to the few people from Saudi he was still in contact with. We got a list of names and addresses, and I wrote to them, explaining that I was looking for my friends. Most of them wanted to help, and they gave me more names and addresses. I wrote every single one of them. I didn't hear anything for a few months, but then I got a letter from a guy who knew Stacy's parents. He gave me their address and number.

"She wasn't very happy to hear from me, and when I told her I was looking for you, she refused to help. I didn't give up, though. I kept writing people. A month later, Stacy called me and apologized. She said she'd try to help, but she didn't know where anyone was. I spoke to her dad and told him what I was trying to do, and he agreed to help, too. A couple of months later, Stacy called and said she had found London. A few months later we found Avery. But she didn't know where anyone was, either. I talked to her dad, too, and he said he'd help out. I didn't hear from him for a while, and I started to lose hope. But then one day Avery called. She said her dad had tracked down a friend who knew Anna's parents. So I called her and found out that she's been in contact with you all this time."

I took that all in, impressed and touched that Alex had tried so hard to find me. That had to mean something. I was important enough to him that he spent an entire year looking for me. "Anna never said anything to me."

"I asked her not to," he said. "I wanted to see you face-to-face first. When she told me that she was going to visit you, I asked her if I could come with her."

"Did you drive with her?"

"No. I flew into Raleigh yesterday and took a bus here. Anna picked me up at my hotel this morning." He paused, his eyes still on me. "I needed to see you, Chloe. There's something I need to say to you."

"Stop," I said. "Don't say anything, Alex. Not yet. There's something you need to see first. Wait here."

In the nursery, I found Anna holding Tyler and making baby talk to him.

"Oh, Chloe," she said. "He's so cute."

Tyler wasn't cranky, which meant he hadn't fallen asleep yet. "Thank you. Let me have him."

Once I had Tyler in my arms, Anna said, "I didn't tell him about Tyler. I didn't think it was my place."

"Thank you."

I walked back to the living room preparing for what I was about to say. How things would be between Alex and me going forward depended on how he reacted. Would he be upset? Would this be too much for him to accept? Would he leave?

I stood in front of Alex for a few moments, holding Tyler in my arms as he studied Alex intently. I drew in a breath. "This is Tyler," I said.

Alex looked at me, confusion on his face. "Are you babysitting?"

"He's my son, Alex. Your son."

Alex looked back at me, his face blank. He looked at Tyler, then back at me. He blinked once. Twice. A third time. He looked from me to Tyler several more times, and I could see a storm of emotion in his eyes. Then understanding came to him, and he swallowed hard.

"My ... son?" he asked in wonder. "I'm a father?"

"Yes, Alex. You're a father."

Alex sat silently, a stunned look on his face, and I could almost see reality sinking in. He slowly stood, then walked over to us, his eyes never leaving Tyler. "I ... can I hold him?"

"Yes." I held Tyler out to him, and he carefully took him into his arms, holding him like he was the most precious thing in the world. Tyler was calm in his arms, seeming not to care that a stranger was holding him.

Alex gazed at Tyler in wonder and amazement.

Tyler looked back at him and reached out to grab at Alex's face. Alex made a little laugh, then looked at me. "He's beautiful," he said, his voice breaking, as a tear rolled down his cheek. "Hi, Tyler. I guess I'm your daddy."

I let out the breath that I'd been holding as relief came over me. "He has your eyes," I said.

Alex didn't take his eyes off of Tyler. "This ... this is pretty crazy. I wasn't sure what to expect when I came here, but it certainly wasn't this. But ..." Now he turned his attention to me, his eyes wet and a smile on his face. "I'm ... amazed. And kind of scared shitless. This is going to change everything." He smiled at me again.

That was what I needed to hear. If he was scared, if he realized everything would change for him, that meant that he was already thinking about the future and his part in Tyler's life. That was reassuring.

Tyler began to squirm, wanting to be put down.

I took Tyler from Alex. "Let's sit," I said, moving to the sofa. I sat Tyler down next to me and gave him a toy bear to keep him occupied. "I need to say something."

Alex sat next to me, his attention still on Tyler, who dropped his bear to look back at Alex. Then Alex grabbed the bear and held it to Tyler, shaking it a little bit to get his attention. Tyler squealed in delight, grabbed the bear, and then, to my surprise, crawled on Alex's lap. Alex beamed, looking so happy.

I remembered back to when I had first met him, and how he had played with the two kids I was babysitting. I guess I shouldn't have been surprised that Tyler had taken to him. Alex's charisma even drew babies in.

"What is it?" he asked.

I waited until he looked at me. I took in a deep breath. "I'm a mother now. Tyler is my life. Everything I do, I do with him in mind. He's the most important thing in my life, and his well-being will always be my top priority. I would sacrifice anything for him. He comes first. Always. I need you to understand this."

Alex's eyes were intense as he listened. He was silent for a few moments, his gaze fixed on me. Then he spoke. "I understand, Chloe. I get it. And I think that makes you an amazing mom."

Despite myself, I smiled.

Tyler slid off Alex's lap to the floor and held himself upright, his hands balancing him against the coffee table. I could tell he was thinking about trying to walk on his own. Sometimes he would pull himself up on something, then let go for a few seconds, but he never took any steps. I knew he was working up the courage.

I wondered if that's how Alex felt right now.

"What did you come here to tell me?" I asked him.

"I ..." he laughed quietly. "I've rehearsed this in my head about a thousand times, but now that I'm here with you ... I'm not sure why this is so hard. It's just three words. It should be easy. I guess I'm scared."

I was right. "Of what? What are you afraid of?"

"That you won't say what I hope you'll say." His eyes never left mine, and I could see the resolve building in them. "I still love you," he said quietly. "I never stopped loving you, Chloe. I told you that you were my one thing, and that's still true. It's just you. Only you. I feel incomplete without you. That's what I've wanted to say to you for over a year. That's why I spent so much time trying to find you. It's because I love you."

I looked back at him, stunned, elation filling me. I couldn't believe it. He still loved me? He spent an entire year looking for me so he could tell me he loved me? I wanted to jump up and down in happiness. I wanted to jump into his arms and kiss him. I wanted to tell him that I felt the same way, that I never stopped loving him either.

But I couldn't. I had to think of Tyler. It had been one thing to fantasize about being with Alex, having him be in my life like I'd always wanted him to, but with the reality of him sitting on my sofa, I had to think of Tyler first.

I forced myself to remain calm. "Alex ... what you just said ... it makes me happy. It makes me really happy. And that's because I still love you too. My feelings for you haven't changed. I want you to know that."

Alex's face brightened.

"But I can't just jump into a relationship with you again. Things are different now. I have Tyler."

He nodded. "I understand," he said. "I'm just happy to hear you say that you still love me. But I'm not going to lie to you. I want to be with you, Chloe. I want us to have the chance that we didn't get that summer. But I'm not going to pressure you. I understand that you might need to time to figure things out. And if you decide that there's no room in your life for me ... I'll respect your decision."

He got it. He really got it. I smiled at him. "Thank you, Alex." I reached out and touched his arm. "It means a lot to me to hear you say that. We'll talk later. I need to think about things. Give me some time, okay?"

He nodded again, and smiled his wonderful smile at me. "Okay."

Then we were silent as we continued to watch each other.

"So ..." he said, breaking our spell.

"Let me put Tyler down," I said, still smiling. "He needs his nap. Then you, me and Anna can talk. We all have some catching up to do."

CHAPTER TWENTY-TWO

The three of us talked nonstop, but the conversation centered on Alex. It was mostly for my benefit, as Alex and Anna had already talked a few times on the phone.

Alex was living in Maryland near DC since he left Saudi and had just graduated from high school. He was starting college in the fall at the University of Maryland, and he wanted to major in electrical engineering. I was impressed that he had built a new life for himself, and appeared to be doing well.

When Anna asked him if he'd had a girlfriend, he looked right at me, and he said he hadn't. He was trying to tell me that he only wanted to be with me, and he'd been loyal to my memory. That made me feel good. When he asked about me, and I said I hadn't had a boyfriend, he looked so relieved it made me smile. I liked that he would have been jealous if I had been with someone.

Alex asked all about my pregnancy, and what my

life had been like since Tyler was born. I didn't hold back. I didn't sugarcoat anything. He never interrupted me, and I knew he understood that my life had been hard in part because he hadn't been around to help me.

After a couple of hours, I asked Anna to take Alex back to his hotel. Mom would be back soon, and I didn't want Alex to be in the house when she got back. I didn't know how she'd react. I'd told her about Alex's role in his girlfriend's death, and how he had struggled with guilt that summer. She understood why Alex had tried to kill himself. I knew that she felt for Alex. But I also knew she was angry at him for what he had done, and for how badly it had affected me.

She'd have to see him at some point, but I didn't want it to be today. I had to talk to her first.

That night, I left Anna in the guest room playing with Tyler. Dad was out with his Air Force buddies watching a baseball game, so I could talk to Mom alone. She was in the kitchen, loading the dishwasher.

"Mom?" I stood in the doorway.

She turned to look at me. "Yes, honey?"

"I need to talk to you about something."

She looked at me for a few moments, then sighed. "You know it makes me nervous when you say that."

"Don't worry," I said. "It's nothing bad."

"Okay ... what is it?"

"I saw Alex today." It was best just to get it out there. "Anna brought him over."

Mom didn't say anything. She wiped her hands

dry, then rubbed lotion into them.

I waited.

"I see," she finally said, and I could see the conflicting emotions on her face. She was concerned for me. She was angry on my behalf. But she knew how much I'd wanted Alex to be a part of my life. She never said it, but I knew she knew I still loved him. "And how is he?"

"He's good, Mom. He's all better now."

"You told him about Tyler?"

"Yes."

"And how did he take it?"

I'd been thinking about that all evening. Alex had taken the news that he was a father so much better than I had imagined. "He took it really well. He was surprised at first, naturally, but he seemed really happy, Mom. He said he wants to be involved, and I think he really meant it."

"Are you sure?" she asked, moving to stand close to me.

"Yes, Mom, I am."

"It's been so long. What does he want? Why did he come?"

I couldn't help but blush. "To tell me he still loves me. He said he wants to be with me again."

She was silent, probably skeptical. "I see," she said again. "And you said?"

"I told him I loved him too."

"Chloe ... you're almost seventeen. I know you've

matured, but this is a big deal. You need to realize that how you decide to handle this can potentially affect the rest of your life. You have to think of Tyler."

I was tempted to roll my eyes at her. I'd proven to her over and over that Tyler was the most important thing in my world. I'd given up having friends. I'd given up activities that I'd always been part of. I had no social life because all of my free time was devoted to Tyler. But I understood that she couldn't help worrying. That's just what mothers do.

"That's exactly what I told Alex." I recounted what I'd said, and how he'd reacted.

"But he hurt you, honey. I know that he was in pain. I know that he felt responsible for that girl's death. How do we know he won't hurt you again? Can we trust him?"

I loved how she said *we*. "I've thought about that too, and I do trust him. He's doing really well, Mom. He has his life all together now. I trust him. And now he can be part of Tyler's life. Tyler can have a father now. And that's something I can't ignore. Don't you think it would be a good thing for Tyler to have a father?"

Mom let out a resigned sigh. "I do. I think that's a very good thing. And I know that you've ... that you've missed him. Tell me what you want to do."

"I'm not sure," I said. "I told him I had to think about it, and he said he'd wait. And he said he'd respect my decision if I told him I didn't want to be with him again. But, Mom, you should have seen how he was with Tyler. You should have seen how he played with him. He was so good with him."

Again, Mom was silent as she considered my words. She stepped away from me, taking off her apron. "I want to talk with him. I'm sure your dad has some things to say too. Will he be by tomorrow?"

"Yes. He's staying at a hotel. Anna's going to go get him in the morning. Then you can talk to him. But, Mom ... "

"Yes?"

"Just you first. I don't want Dad to scare him away."

Anna went to get Alex as soon as Tyler was finished with breakfast.

As we waited, I got more and more nervous. What was Mom going to say to Alex?

When he arrived, Alex was very polite, and Mom was trying to be friendly and welcoming. But there was no small talk. We sat in the living room, and Mom began her interrogation. She never mentioned anything about Alex's suicide attempt or asked about what he'd been doing the past two years. Her questions were all about Tyler and me.

"What are your intentions, Alex?" she asked him pointedly.

Alex didn't hesitate. "I want to be part of Tyler's

life, and I want to be with Chloe. I want to do this together with her."

I wasn't expecting that, and I don't think Mom was either. I couldn't help but feel touched by his words. To hear him say that with such conviction made me feel better about all of this.

"And how do you intend to do that if you're going to be in college in Maryland?

"Well, ma'am, I'm eighteen now. I don't need anyone's permission to do what I want. I can move here."

"And how will you support yourself? Are you assuming your parents will continue to pay for your expenses? Forgive me, but I find that naïve and unrealistic. You have no money and no way to support yourself."

"No, ma'am. You're right. But I've already spoken to my parents, and they said that they would support me. They want to help. They want me to be a part of Tyler's life, too. They want me to help Chloe."

That surprised me. That his parents felt that way, after just having found out about Tyler, made me feel so relieved. I had been worried about how they would take the news.

"But you need to realize that this will change your life forever," Mom said. "Are you prepared for that? Are you willing to give up the life you have now to be Tyler's father?"

Alex's resolve shown on his face. "I am. I've been

looking for Chloe for a year. She's all I've been thinking of. I love your daughter, and if she'll have me, I'll be part of her life for as long as she wants me. Honestly, I don't really have much of a life to give up. I don't have friends. I'm not involved with anything that I would miss. My life since I've gotten better has been all about finding Chloe. She's what I want."

I couldn't help it. Hearing Alex say these things made the love I still felt for him fill me to the point that I started to cry. Anna scooted close to me and put her arm around me.

Mom wasn't through. "What about college? Frankly, I don't want Chloe starting a life with someone without a college education."

Alex didn't back down. "I can withdraw from the University of Maryland, and attend a school here, even a community college. I'll find a job to cover my rent, and my parents offered to use what they save in tuition to help us." It didn't escape me that he'd said *us*. "I'll stay here until Chloe graduates and goes to college. Then I'll go with her."

Mom pursed her lips, then put her hands flat on her thighs. "Well, Alex, I can see that you've given this a lot of thought, but following through is much more difficult than making plans."

Alex glanced at me, then spoke to my mother. "I understand that you have concerns. I know that ... I know that you have no reason to trust me. But I'm very serious about this. I spent a solid year getting myself straightened out, and in the back of my mind the whole time was the hope that I could find Chloe again. I love her."

"Are you going to marry her?" Mom said suddenly, and my eyebrows shot up in surprise. *Marry me?*

"If and when she's ready."

I was so shocked to hear that, I actually gasped. I wanted to run to him, hold him, kiss him.

"You're Tyler's father," Mom said. "And if this is what Chloe wants, then I won't get in the way." She stood. "I'm glad you're doing well, Alex."

"Thank you, ma'am."

Mom left us in the living room, and we all sat there without speaking. My sniffling was the only sound.

When I swallowed the lump in my throat, I managed to speak. "Do you really mean all that, Alex? Would you really give up your life for Tyler and me?"

He nodded and smiled at me, his blue eyes full of promise. "In a heartbeat, Chloe. If you want me, I'll do whatever it takes to be with you. I will leave everything behind to start a new life with you. I promise you I won't run away. I won't leave you and Tyler."

"I ... I don't know what to say." I really didn't. I knew what I *wanted* to say. I wanted Alex in my life again. I wanted to be with him again. Everything he had said, the conviction and confidence in his voice, it had all given me a hope I never thought I could feel. And I selfishly wanted to have a partner, someone to help me raise Tyler. But, even more than that, I wanted Tyler to have a father who was involved in his life. I wanted Tyler to grow up with two parents who loved him.

This was too good to be true. I couldn't quite make myself believe that this could happen.

Alex waited patiently while I gathered my thoughts.

"Alex ... I want you to know that I love you. You're the only person I've ever loved, and I will always love you, no matter what happens between us. And ... I believe that you love me. And that Tyler is important to you. But ... I can't rush into anything with you, no matter how much I want it. And I do want it, Alex. I really do. I just ... I just need time. Is that okay? Will you wait for me?"

He smiled, his beautiful eyes bright. "I'll wait for you, Chloe. I'll always wait for you."

I wiped the tears from my cheeks, then smiled at him. I stood. "Come on." I held my hand out to him and pulled him up. "Let's have some lunch and then we can catch up some more. I have so much to tell you."

CHAPTER TWENTY-THREE

I waited in the hotel room. Mom, Aunt Kelly and London had just left, leaving me alone with Anna. She sat on the sofa, watching me as I paced. I was too worked up to sit.

"Are you nervous?" she asked. "You look nervous."

A hysterical little laugh escaped me. "Like crazy. I can't believe this is about to happen. I feel ... am I too young for this, Anna?"

"You're eighteen now. You're a legal adult."

"I know ... I'm just—"

"Scared," Anna supplied. "Which is totally okay. It's a big step, but I know you're ready for this. Trust me. Every time you've talked to me about this, you've been so excited I thought you might explode."

"You're right. I'm just being crazy. Do I look okay?"

She smiled. "Chloe, you look beautiful. You're stunning."

I continued pacing, careful not to step on my dress. Tripping and ripping it was the last thing I needed. "What if Alex backs out?"

"He moved here to be with you, Chloe. He gave up a place at a good, four-year school to go to a community college for you. That's a huge sacrifice. He's a good guy. Even your dad can't stop telling everyone how great Alex is."

That was true. When I first told my dad Alex had come to see me, he'd freaked out and told me flat out that he didn't want me involved with him at all. But when Alex moved down to be close to me and started being a part of my life and Tyler's life, Dad began to see that Alex was totally committed. Then, two months later, I decided I wanted to be a couple with Alex. Dad saw how happy I was. His attitude toward Alex began to soften, and after a few months, Alex totally won him over. Now, Dad loved Alex just as much as Mom and I did.

"Okay," I said. "I'm just being a spaz." I was just nervous. Alex wouldn't leave Tyler and me. He had proven over and over again that he was totally devoted to us. He was always at my house, helping in any way he could. He babysat all the time to give me the chance to go out to movies and dinner with my mom. He eased my burden, and always made me feel like I had a partner, that I wasn't alone. He was always there for me

No Alex wouldn't leave

I wouldn't have said yes if I doubted even a tiny bit that he would

"Are you looking forward to being with him at State?"

"Yes " Alex and I had both been accepted to North Carolina State University, and our parents were going to help with tuition We'd have to work while we went to school to cover our expenses, but we'd never be able to pay tuition on our own I'd been against that arrangement at first because our parents had already done so much for us I felt bad about them supporting us for another four years, even with the loans we had But they had made it clear that they wanted each of us to have a college education, and that they were committed to helping us "We still have to work out our housing situation It looks like we'll have to rent an apartment off campus " Normally, freshmen had to live on campus, but the school had special rules for situations like ours "We're driving down next week to check things out "

"Well, I'll help you guys when I can," Anna said "I'm going to be really busy with soccer, but I'll make time to babysit when you need me I'll be there for you guys " Anna had a full soccer scholarship at NCSU, and her parents had been all for her attending, even if she'd be out of state They knew that North Carolina State was a good school and had one of the best women's soccer programs in the country

I suspected, though, that Anna's top motivation was for us to go to the same college I was very happy about that Anna was my best friend Being apart for the last three years had been hard, especially since I didn't have any other friends Not real ones Not like when we were in Taif I was so happy that we'd be together again

"Please stop pacing," Anna said "I'm getting a headache watching you "

"Sorry It's just   "

"I know, I know " She smiled and tucked a loose strand of hair behind her ear "Today is a big day for you "

It wasn't just a big day It was the biggest day of my life

Today my life would change forever

There was a knock on the door, and the coordinator stuck her head into the room "They're ready for you," she said

It was time

Anna stood and came close "Come on You'll do fine "

I held my left hand up and looked at my engagement ring, thinking back to that summer when Alex and I had met I remembered our message to each other: *This is me*

After today, Alex and I would have a new message *This is us.*

Printed in Great Britain
by Amazon